HOLD MY PLACE

CASSONDRA WINDWALKER

ISBN print - 9781645481003
ISBN ebook - 9781645480327

Cover Design and Interior Formatting
by Qamber Designs and Media

Published by Black Spot Books,
An imprint of Vesuvian Media Group

For the Cait-Shìth, the Harpies, for the hungry Ammit,
the Rusalki, the Leannán Sidhe, the Erinyes, the Selkies,
and all other dangerous lovers.

BOOKS BY CASSONDRA WINDWALKER

Bury the Lead
Preacher Sam
Idle Hands

No one realizes the words *love never dies* are a curse, not a happy ending. Curses, like the soul, are heavier than the flesh.

PROLOGUE

Have you ever found yourself seized by the compulsion to open your car door while flying down the highway? Ever stared at the door handle, listened to the rumble of tires, the roar of the wind, and wanted more than anything to slip off your seatbelt, fling the door open, and launch yourself out?

Ever stood on the edge of a cliff and peered over into the empty air, wondered what it would feel like if you plunged into the crevasse?

There's no turning back from an indulgence like that. There's the wild liberty, the rush of extravagant recklessness, the communion with the wind. And then, there's death. You can't step back from such an experience. You have to commit.

"I love you so much, Edgar," I whispered.

His eyes softened. His lips curved. And I committed.

I plunged the knife into his belly.

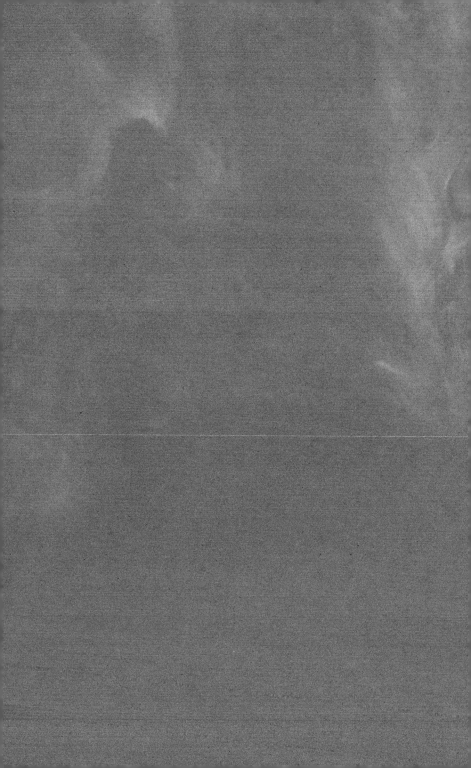

CHAPTER ONE

I remember his first breath on my body. Sweet and warm with port wine, his words skated over the little hairs on the back of my neck, tumbled down my collar.

The master chef whose cooking class I had taken plucked the sticky mess from my hands. I laughed nervously, flushed with heat from my inexpert efforts to properly knead the dough.

"Like this," he said.

A month ago, the library board had held its annual Christmas dinner at *La Table*, the gourmet French-Asian restaurant food bloggers kept raving about. The chef had come out to say good night and accept our accolades, and the moment I saw him, my fork became heavy in my hand. I lost all desire for food. My gaze clung to the curve of his lips, the sharp line of his clean-shaven jaw, the long lock of dark hair lying against the taut muscle of his neck. He voiced some sort of pleasantries, but I didn't hear a word. His left ring finger, dark against his kitchen whites, gleamed with gold, and I sucked in a breath, feeling robbed.

I was hardly a shrinking violet—even in library circles, throwback goths covered in red and black tattoos tended to garner some attention—but that night, I might as well have been invisible. His eyes met everyone's but mine. Afterward, the chef returned to the kitchen, while I didn't take another bite, woodenly contributing as little conversation as necessary until I could make my escape. Instead of calling a car, I'd walked home, stomping through slushy snow and willing my heated skin to cool.

I'd lain awake until the wee hours, the bottle of wine by my bed serving no purpose but to enflame the wicked thoughts confusing me even as they consumed me. I was no girl, flush with infatuation. I was a woman, perfectly content alone—particularly if the alternative was the mewling artifice I'd watched so many of my friends adopt, pretending at weakness and softness to accommodate the egos of their partners. Male or female, it didn't matter. Someone who wasn't powerful always seemed to want to be, so the cost of their companionship was high. Or I might be too frugal, but at any rate, I refused to pet and stroke a fat barn cat and call it a tiger.

Nor had I ever been one of those women who craved the illicit, chasing after self-proclaimed bad boys and semi-committed men. I tended to be too pragmatic for secret love affairs. When the whole relationship is predicated on the fact the other person can't be trusted, I think it puts a dampener on things. And it's way too much work. All those lies and excuses and late-night assignations. I need my beauty sleep. The library opens at nine sharp every morning, and while I could probably be persuaded to stay up late for a thousand-year-old vampire lover or a banished Norse god, anything less just doesn't tempt me.

I have a weakness for paranormal romance. So what? Librarians have the most degenerate taste in literature there is. Why do you think we're forever trumpeting the cause of banned books?

All this simply to say my brain should have relegated this beautiful man to the uninteresting column almost immediately.

Instead, I lay sweating under the ka-thumping ceiling fan, fingers plucking at hot, slick skin beneath tangled sheets, the uncoiling release of my flesh only wrenching tighter the anguished anticipation of my soul. He was mine, something whispered harshly in the back of my mind, he was mine first, even though God knows I'd never seen him before.

The next morning, I took a hot shower before work and told myself I was washing the night away, but thoughts of the man intruded again and again. When I found the gourmet cooking class advertised for February, I ripped out the newspaper page and balled it up. Fully intending to toss it.

But I stuck it in my pocket.

Here I am, two weeks later, abusing beignet dough in a class of nine other no doubt equally infatuated women. How humiliating.

When Evan, my coworker and friend, asked why I'd signed up for cooking classes when I fed myself nachos and burritos six nights a week—a woman needs one night reserved for martinis—I'd claimed it was my foray into the dating scene. That I'd rather meet a man who I knew could cook than find someone online or in a bar. I was glad Evan couldn't see me now. With not an eligible man in sight, he'd never let me hear the end of it. Based on the amount of cleavage and red lipstick on display, the other students suffered from the same malady as I did where Chef Edgar was concerned.

Edgar Leyward was his name.

I'd never known an Edgar before. Kind of an old-fashioned name, like Harold or Frank or Herbert. His angular bone structure reminded me of fabled giants and begged me to draw my fingers over the bladed edges of his face. His dusky skin tone, slightly darker than mine even in this clime of perpetual rain and gray skies, evoked the Northwestern tribes I'd come to associate with this part of the coastline but could have easily been credited to the Mediterranean or the South American continent. His name gave no clues, nor did the cuisine of the French fusion restaurant his creations had boosted from middling to sublime.

At that moment, though, I focused on the hypnotic rhythm of

his long fingers, dusted with flour, working the tender, sticky dough. "You're not punishing the dough," he told me, his voice husky with equal parts restrained impatience and laughter. "You're summoning the beignets."

Handsome he might be, but apparently still as pretentious as any French chef worthy of the name, I thought. "Like a demon?" I asked, not bothering to hide my own amusement.

"Like a lover," he told me. Though, he didn't bother to cast a glance my way, I could feel myself flush to the roots of my black hair. "Like a lover who has forgotten your name and your face, who can only recognize you by your hands on their body."

He ruined the effect by throwing a broad wink at the student across the table from me, who had stopped kneading and was watching him open-mouthed. He thrust my dough back at me.

"Just don't beat it half to death," he concluded. "You'll make the bread tough instead of flaky."

My classmate—the 'Hello my name is', sticker on her T-shirt identified her as Tiffany—pulled herself together with a visible effort and commenced folding and pressing her dough.

"Well worth the price of admission," Tiffany murmured, casting me a conspiratorial glance.

I shrugged, trying to forget how my whole body had gone cold beneath his breath, even as my heart thudded nearly out of my chest. "If you go for the oversexed malcontent type," I muttered back.

She laughed out loud, drawing the gazes of the other eight students in the room. "Who doesn't?"

I don't, I grumpily thought, giving the dough a good whack out of sheer contrariness. Suddenly I was well and truly ashamed of myself for even signing up for this class. I could hardly disdain Tiffany for her crush when my whole reason for being here was clearly the same as hers.

I smiled slightly, and congratulated myself on my black denim overalls and white tank top that displayed my degenerate status but none of my cleavage. Several of the sleekly coiffed students had stared askance at the Celtic animals and Norse gods swarming my bare arms. At least I was less obvious than them.

I hoped.

Needless to say, my beignets turned out on the stony side of soft. I told myself I didn't care. After all, as far as I was concerned, the whole purpose of beignets was to draw me out of the house, not trap me in the kitchen. A steaming pastry, a cup of spicy black tea, and the merry bustle of a street corner café was my idea of a perfect morning. Still, I swallowed an unexpected lump of jealousy as Edgar exclaimed over some other tart's perfect flaky sweet.

I laughed at my pun and then choked on air, being the graceful creature of mystery I am. My hacking drew the chef's attention, and he stared down at my little pasty squares of concrete with undisguised dismay.

"Oh," was all he could summon up after wrenching off a corner and chewing it with what I felt was an unnecessary exaggeration of force.

I shrugged. "Slap a little Nutella on those babies, they'll be delicious. I could even take the leftovers to work. The guys will love them."

I could have sworn I saw tears of restrained laughter in his golden-brown eyes. I'd never seen eyes quite that color. I should have dismissed them as boring old brown, but they were shot through with light, like sunlight behind a shattered piece of amber.

"Will they?" he asked dubiously, swallowing with effort.

"Of course, they will. Everything's better with Nutella."

He simply nodded, no doubt thinking if this crazy woman was happy with what she paid for, he wasn't about to argue. He continued with his review of the students' work, refilling wine glasses and sharing tips as we packed up our food and got ready to head home.

"Next week, we'll be making duck a l'orange with a bit of Chinese flair."

Now, libraries are fiercely organized realms. Have you ever

noticed how many decimal places can stretch out to the right in the Dewey Decimal system? Not to mention how anal we are when it comes to alphabetizing. A place for everything and everything in its place is the rule of law in a library, which naturally requires me to be completely scattered in every other aspect of my life. There was absolutely nothing deliberate about the fact I was the last one to gather up all my stuff and cram it into my black leather shoulder bag. Absolutely nothing.

Not that Edgar seemed to notice. He was cleaning up with his back to me. I clacked past him in my clunky boots, and he called me back as I reached the door.

"Sigrun."

Impossibly, I felt his tongue shape my name. I froze and forgot to breathe. I wanted him to say it again.

And he did.

"Sigrun, stay. Have another glass of wine with me."

CHAPTER TWO

I could have told myself a few more minutes in each other's company was perfectly innocuous. After all, we'd all been drinking wine together during the cooking class. What would one more glass and a few minutes of conversation hurt?

But when I steeled myself to look straight into those amber eyes and say yes, the rush of hunger suffusing me made the lie impossible. More than simple lust, it was an ache, a terrible longing to lay my hands not only on his body but on his soul. I lowered my gaze, quelling a shudder. I had no hope of him not seeing the wild avarice in my eyes.

He didn't open another of the bottles of port standing on the counter. Instead, he took my elbow and guided me out of the kitchen, into the dim sconce-lit dining room of the restaurant proper. Chairs splayed their legs indecently atop the intimate tables, and all but the sidelights were turned off. Edgar seated me at the bar.

I placed my palms on the gleaming walnut wood and willed my blood to slow its mad rampaging through my veins. From behind the bar, Edgar poured a glass of Burgundy wine for each of us before coming back around to sit beside me.

I wrapped both hands around the crystal and sipped slowly, already covetous of these brief moments we'd stolen. The rich liquid slid down my throat, and I imagined that one of Edgar's long, broad fingers traced its path on my skin.

I might have been content to simply sit there a long time, lost in the rhythm of his breath, in the faint warmth emanating from his thigh resting so near mine, but he wanted more.

"So, Sigrun. Are you a librarian or merely on the board?"

My eyes widened. "You—you know who I am? You saw me?" I could have sworn his eyes hadn't rested on me that night four—or was it five?—weeks ago for an instant.

He laughed low. "Who could miss you?"

I quirked my brows. Fair point, but he'd done a damn fine job of pretending otherwise. I hadn't caught even the slightest flicker of recognition when I showed up in his class tonight.

"Librarian," I conceded. "Do I strike you as a board member?"

Another laugh.

I decided I would happily make twelve kinds of a fool of myself to keep hearing that sound.

"Hey, the times, they are a-changing, you know. Believe me, nobody who looks like you worked in the library when I was a kid."

"To be fair, I kind of snookered them," I confessed. "I wore long sleeves to all my interviews, and I may have toned down the makeup a bit." I batted the thick fake lashes glittering with tiny crystals. "And wearing black to an interview is pretty much expected. They just didn't know it was the primary color in my closet."

"I can't imagine them being disappointed."

"Well, I've been working there for six years now, so they must be reasonably satisfied by my skills. And honestly, all the stereotypes about librarians couldn't be more misunderstood. We're all nonconformists." I warmed to my topic and the wine. "People forget when the tired old trope of the spinster librarian was trotted out, being a spinster *was* an act of revolt. A woman who chose learning over a man? Shocking! And the only way men could justify that possibility was to give her Coke-bottle glasses and a hairy wart."

Edgar chuckled softly, his eyes following my mouth as I spoke. "I can see you haven't devoted any thought to this at all. But no Coke bottles for you."

I shrugged. "Actually, I'm blind as a bat. I wear contacts most of the time, but if you saw me with my glasses on, you'd concede I meet the requirements. I keep my warts shaved, though."

This time, he laughed out loud. "Thank God."

"What about you? How long have you been at *La Table*?" I set my wine glass down a bit too hard. "Scratch that. I don't really care. What I want to know is why you're drinking and talking here with me instead of with your wife."

Yes, I favor the direct approach. Life is short. I wasn't inclined to pretend, even to myself, that I was unaware of what was happening.

He didn't look surprised, though, or even taken aback. He glanced at the worn gleam on his finger then back at me without flinching.

"It's a strange thing, isn't it?"

"No," I protested. "Not really. What could be more predictable than a man who cheats?"

He nodded.

I found myself growing perturbed at his apparent inability to take offense. Weren't chefs supposed to be notoriously temperamental?

"I've loved my wife longer than I can say," Edgar said. "That will never change. I don't know who I am without her. But I needed to talk to you. No. More than that. I needed to connect with you. Tell me you don't feel the same."

Less than an inch separated my hand from his on the bar. I wanted to yank my hands away, to look away, walk away.

But away was a circle, not a line, and everything in me that screamed *run* as quickly screamed *run back*.

"I—I don't know," I lied.

"Don't you?" he asked softly.

He could have left me there in my indecision and hypocrisy, but he didn't. Instead, he stood, swept away our glasses, and returned the bottle of wine. He held out his hand to me.

"Let's go for a walk."

"I think it's snowing," I said.

"So, we'll get cold."

When I recount this first night of ours to myself, I sometimes like to pretend I could have refused him. I could have waved goodbye, even chanced the temptation of a kiss on the cheek, and walked home alone. But truly, I think it was already too late. His gaze, his voice, even the unfulfilled promise of his touch, were a drug. Rules, laws, ethics, human decency—none of them seemed to matter, or even exist. All that was real was his breath drifting toward me, his hand reaching out for me.

Something skittered through my veins then, something darker than blood, swifter than thought, colder than a corpse. Something urging me closer, even as it pulled me further away from myself.

I offered no objection. I only wanted to stand under the umbrella of his eyes, let his voice rain down around our tiny respite and keep the world at bay.

I took his hand.

His warmth enveloped me. For a scant instant, my knees weakened. Every nerve tingled, and I almost fancied my spirit bursting past my skin and hovering there. Then, with a gust of desire, I whooshed fully back into my bones. Back into my want.

We walked.

Not much of a torrid affair. It felt more like a ghost story as we shuffled along the empty, icy sidewalks, our only point of contact our cold, mittenless hands. Nearly midnight on a weeknight, and every silhouette was a shade of gray, from the austere faces of the buildings to the arrested sculptures to the sleet-cloaked streetlights. I couldn't say what we talked about as we tromped on, huddled against the wind in our puffy parkas, or if we talked at all. We stopped at a gray fountain, its water drained for winter, and gazed at its starless basin as if we searched for pennies and their wishes. I'm not sure how we wound up at my apartment stairs.

I must have led us there, but my heart still sank when I recognized the address.

Edgar turned me to face him. His right hand, so icy cold, rested against my cheek. He didn't say a word, only dropped the faintest kiss on my forehead, and strode into the enveloping night.

I mounted the steps to my apartment as if I were in a trance, half-frozen and unable to think past the bare brush of his lips on my skin. The door slid open beneath my fingers, though I had no memory of reaching for the keys. A wave of dizziness blurred my vision, and I clung to the doorframe as though the void of darkness at my back might suck me into a night I could not escape. When my eyes cleared, a new terror seized my throat. Where was I? Whose home was this? What were these candles, these books, these strange paintings with their staring eyes? Who was I?

I dared not step back, dared not even look into the blackness behind me. So, I stepped forward, closed the door as if it were my own. A voice inside this skin whispered softly, *"Sigrun,"* and the panic subsided.

Still, I lay that night in a stranger's bed, staring up at her ceiling until dreams pulled me swiftly into a black river. Everything had changed.

CHAPTER THREE

'd been wrong to think there were no rules between us. Somehow, without a moment's discussion, they sprang into effect as comfortable and familiar as an old cardigan.

Every night at eleven, I stood in the alley behind *La Table* like some mobster's sad doxy.

I wished I smoked cigarettes. One of those lovely long cigarette holders and a thin curl of smoke wisping up from my shadow would have added powerfully to the effect. Sadly, I limited my vices to too much eyeshadow and not quite enough vodka, so I lost out on the potential dramatics.

Edgar would emerge from the back door, lit up for an instant in the kitchen fluorescence. At the sight of him, my gut would clench, my breath stutter. Then the door would close, and unerringly he would reach me in the blackness. The other kitchen staff did the cleaning up, so we were alone as we began our nightly amble.

I still don't know if we were going somewhere or not. To a bystander's eyes, we must have looked aimless, just two people walking up and down the streets until exhaustion drove us to part at my apartment steps, by whatever circuitous route we had taken. Sometimes, though, I felt a strange desperation pulling at my skin, nipping at my heels as if what looked like a stroll was a frantic search. As if there were some hidden door after which all our consciousness yearned, and night after night, we sought its frame.

But we found no door.

Unaccustomed to these late nights, I began to feel rather haggard. Happily haggard is a perfectly acceptable look for a middle-aged goth librarian. I guess thirty-two isn't really middle-aged, but it's definitely not the first bloom of youth, either. I leaned into it, adding extra purple to the shadows under my eyes and painting shattered black cracks onto my cheeks. I was a horror-movie porcelain doll, staring at my reflection with haunted eyes. Evan approved of my new look.

"You're my favorite zombie valentine." Evan laughed.

Sweet Evan couldn't have been more vanilla himself. Born and raised in Oregon, he'd somehow escaped the hipster virus but failed to inoculate himself against basic-boy-next-door. I loved him anyway, damn ballcaps and all.

I must have looked horrified because Evan laughed. "Here." He hastily cut out a ragged red heart from the children's librarian's construction paper stash. He pinned it to my black suspenders. "Now you're valentine ready."

I recovered quickly and harrumphed in his general direction. "Valentine's Day isn't exactly my on-brand holiday," I told him.

Inwardly, though, I felt a swell of panic. Damn Hallmark and their never-ending cheer. Tonight was the second night of my cooking class. It occurred to me Edgar might not be there. Would his wife expect him home on Valentine's Day? Did he have some sort of subordinate chef who would take over this class?

And if he was there, how awkward would this be? A swell of fury at commercial expectations hit my chest like a tsunami. It's a lot more comfortable to be mad at big business than to dissect one's own ill-fitting and ill-defined feelings. Maybe I should just skip the class. On principle, I never bought Valentine's Day candy until the day *after* the holiday, because obviously. Who wouldn't want twice the chocolate? But maybe tonight I would make an exception. Fill up on red-foiled decadence at the store and go home to drown my awkwardness in chocolate and Netflix horror movies.

No, I do *not* watch Hallmark movies. A little comic horror, a lot of truffles, and a few dirty martinis should do me nicely.

It was at this point I recognized the true depths of my new depravity. All advantages to the contrary, I could not convince myself to sacrifice the slightest chance of seeing Edgar. Not even for a lapful of confections and a screen splattered with gore.

I could have just texted Edgar, could have asked if he would be at class tonight. Could have sent him some ridiculous Happy Horrible Valentine's Day gif to ease the potential discomfort, but I didn't have his phone number. Nor did he have mine.

One of those strange unspoken rules we navigated. Whatever we were, whatever this was, existed only in those gray sidewalk hours, in the space between our two palms as we walked.

His wife came to class that night. Of course, she did. What wife wouldn't? Not being a fool, she allowed us all our fantasies first. She waited until the lesson was half-done before she came drifting through the door, I swear to God, like fucking Zelda.

She was everything I was not, everything I could never be. I should have expected as much, but somehow, I had the idea we weren't so different. Somehow, I thought we'd share the same dark hair, the same affectation of tossing it over our shoulders. Somehow, I thought I'd see myself in her eyes. Or better yet, my antithesis, some sort of wonderful villain I could loathe and rob without a moment's shame.

Neither were true.

She was tiny. I am best described as a chunk of womanhood. She was short. I am decidedly not. She was ethereally fair. Now, I'll own I'm a dirty blond myself, somewhere deep, deep down under all the black hair dye, but that was our only approximate similarity. Her cropped hair was nearly white, her eyes a wonderful, impossible clear jade green. From the moment I saw her, I fell almost as hard as I'd fallen for Edgar.

I wasn't even sure whether she was walking or floating across the room when she crossed the floor. At first, I thought Edgar wasn't aware of her entrance, thought he was entirely focused on showing Tiffany how to reduce the sauce, but just as she reached him, his bulky arm swept out and lifted her off her feet, bending her over for a ridiculous, exultant kiss. I felt tears rise in my throat, but they weren't tears of jealousy or pain. They were tears of joy.

He hadn't lied. Not in the slightest. He adored her. In that moment, he somehow became her, and I was grateful to have had the chance to see it.

Gradually, I became aware the rest of the class was clapping, and I joined in, awkwardly and too late. It didn't matter. All their focus was on each other, and every other student in the class was as transfixed by them as I was.

"My queen," Edgar presented her to us. "Octavia Leyward. And before you get the wrong idea—I took my name from her, not the other way around. She is the ley line to my eternity."

His words should have cut much deeper than they did. They cut to the bone, but that wasn't deep enough to rob the words of their ecstasy.

She lifted a hand to cup his cheek just as he'd cupped mine a week ago. Only then did I notice the trail of baby roses, palest blush pink, clutched in her hand. A tiny trickle of blood ran down her wrist, but neither of them regarded it.

"Happy day, my love," she whispered, as if none of us were there, as if they weren't standing in a bright white industrial kitchen surrounded by machines and counters and garish lights.

"Happy day," he murmured back.

I turned my head as he pressed his lips to hers in a way he had never pressed his lips to mine.

"It was good to meet you," she said to us before drifting back out like some infernal ghost. She paused at the doorway and turned, and her eyes met mine across the room.

Transparent Jade. Who in the world had eyes like that? I fell into them. It was like falling into a star, when you expected all sound and explosions and flaming fire but found yourself only pierced through with light, the purest, most beloved light.

She smiled.

I choked on a sob as the door closed.

I attempted to return to my tasks at the table, but I had no idea what we were doing. Beating the duck breasts? Making the sauce? Aha. I would just drink the wine. I slurped down tonight's offering—a vapid pinot blanc—and Tiffany eyed me with a skepticism I couldn't ignore.

"Are you even trying?" she asked.

"I don't think so," I confessed. "Is it just me or is this officially now the worst Valentine's Day ever?"

Tiffany shot a glance around the room of dejected, broken-hearted Edgar-hopefuls. She sniffed and nodded decisively.

"Definitely. Worst ever. I mean, the guy's been Forest Glen's hottest man three years in a row. She couldn't even throw us a bone tonight of all nights?"

I should mention, Forest Glen isn't exactly a boom town, and our little town rag couldn't possibly have had a lot of contestants for that position. Between the few men I see at the library and the smarmy faces of realtors and car salesmen splashed on posters all over town, Edgar Leyward had to be kind of a shoo-in.

I shrugged, trying for casual unconcerned. "I guess an alpha wolf's gotta mark her territory, right?"

Damn. Misfire. Tiffany's eyes shot back to me, sharp as blades. "Alpha wolf? That delicate little sprite? Please."

Her tone begged me to say more, but I resisted the impulse. I wouldn't say what I somehow knew: Octavia Leyward was fiercer, more formidable, more fantastic than Tiffany could guess.

Based on what, exactly? Green eyes? A melodramatic kiss, tinged with blood?

Against my better judgment, I twisted on my stool to seek his face. His eyes met mine across the room as if he'd been waiting for me. There, just beneath his cheekbone, a drop of blood from her thorny caress.

Hunger speared through my belly. More than anything, I ached to lick that blood from his skin. Taste its copper bitterness, its regret, its *almost*, warring on my tongue with the warm saltiness of his flesh.

O-kay. Even for a happily dedicated goth, that was a bit on the vampiric side. While I did appreciate the subculture's admirable dedication, it was still only a fanfic fantasy at best. And not one to which I'd ever adhered. I like to *read* about vampires, but I don't want to be responsible for their very inconvenient habits. Plus—shamed as I am to admit it—I tend to gag a bit if the steak's too rare.

I'm sorry! I was born and raised in Kansas, which is cattle country, but some of the dirt just don't stick. I may have a fondness for charred meat and ketchup. What can I say? I've always been on the outside.

Edgar's eyes shifted away, and I felt a sudden absence in my gut. How had I become so bound up by this man in seven short nights? Had it been seven nights? Seven years? Seventy? Scenes of our strange courtship clacked by in my mind like the jerky, blurred images of some old silent movie. I could see Edgar's lips moving as he bent toward me. Had we really shared those streets, those seven nights, or had I only ever been an observer, an interloper, a distant audience?

Seven cold, exhausting nights of snow and sleet and ice and words, words, words.

You know what words are, right? Have you ever thought about it? What a word is? It's a manifestation of the soul, shaped by the most intimate part of the flesh, and made music. Words.

It's God. It's the divine. It's us, at our most elemental.

That's what we were. What we were becoming. Out there on the slush-covered sidewalks, in the gray.

It's what flashed in her eyes when she looked at me in that last goodbye, the only time I would ever see her. The word shared from his lips to hers to my heart.

A word shaped like resurrection, but I shivered with the cold dank of the grave.

CHAPTER FOUR

had no intention of lingering after class. I was sure Edgar and
Octavia had plans, and I wasn't about to humiliate myself by forcing him to tell me so. He must have guessed my resolve because
as I was packing up and chatting to Tiffany with determined cheer, I
felt the pressure of his palm in the small of my back. He kept walking without a pause, but I unslung the bag from my shoulder.

"I think I'll hit the restroom before I walk home," I told Tiffany. "See you next week?"

"Are you kidding?" she asked me. "This class constitutes my
whole social life. I wouldn't miss it. I don't know what I'll do come
March. I think the margarita bar downtown does salsa classes. Maybe I'll give that a try. Be my partner?"

I laughed. "I am your worst possible choice for anything in-
volving grace or balance. You better ask somebody else."

She shrugged, looking mildly disappointed but not surprised.
"Let me know if you change your mind. You could do a whole Day
of the Dead thing, add a little sugar skull to your repertoire."

"I mean, that would work, but I'd probably still break your foot."

"Ooh, downer."

I took my time in the bathroom, and when I emerged, only
Edgar remained in the kitchen classroom. Silently, he helped me
back into my coat and replaced my bag on my shoulder. When we
stepped outside, the day's cold rain had turned into huge, fat snow-
flakes just beginning to collect in heaps on the puddles. Here and

there the faintest sheen of ice stretched over the sidewalks, cob-webbed with tiny cracks.

"I thought you'd be busy tonight," I said, curling my fingers into the warmth of his palm as we walked.

He smiled down at me as if I were the only other person in the world. How was that possible after the exchange he'd had with his wife? And still my heart believed it.

"I am busy," he said. "I'm with you."

It was enough. Well, almost enough.

As we walked and talked about Japanese fairytales and Scandinavian literature and German baking, his nearness became almost excruciating. The slightest rasp of his hand against mine, jostled by our stride, sent hunger and pleasure ribboning through my veins. I watched his breath frost in the air as he spoke and imagined that breath on my bare skin. I lost myself in the timbre and intonations of his voice as if language were his violin. I ached with longing—not like some windswept Brontë heroine, but like a flu patient.

"Come upstairs," I urged him when we reached my steps. Only two words, but they came out in a rush and nearly tumbled over each other.

"Not yet." His voice was a low rumble of yearning and regret.

I wasn't hurt. I knew without the slightest doubt he wanted me. Thinking back to how he looked at me then, how he held my hand like a treasure, I can only say he cherished me. Utterly. So, I wasn't hurt but I was bitterly, bitterly disappointed.

He framed my face in both his hands. "I want you, Sigrun."

Lord, how I loved my name on his tongue.

"When we come together, I want it to be complete. I want to know every corner of your secret self. I want to give you every piece of mine."

I suppose I should have asked how that was possible when Octavia clearly possessed more than just a sliver of his soul, but I didn't. And maybe I should have felt more than a faint frisson of fear, of warning, at such a bald declaration of his intent to trespass, to overwhelm, to own me.

Should have, but didn't.

I nodded dumbly. He dropped his hands from my face and seized my wrists, turning them over and pressing his lips to the blue veins. I shivered and left him there. Alone, I tramped upstairs to my quiet apartment and cold bed.

Our strange routine continued throughout the month. Every day I grew more impatient, but every night he soothed and stoked me with some meager caress—his long fingers trailing on my neck, spearing through my long hair, brushing the heartbeat on my wrist. Even his mouth remained sacrosanct.

Tiffany and I exchanged numbers on the last night of class. I'd originally dismissed her as something of an airhead, a little too bubblegum for me, but she had a kind heart and a great sense of humor. She reminded me of a hamster with her fluffy light brown hair and twitchy nose and weirdly irrepressible cuteness. To be honest, I think she just wore me down. I suspected everyone she spent time with ended up as her friend whether they wanted to be or not. I even grudgingly agreed to accompany her to salsa lessons the next week.

I would miss being in the kitchen with Edgar, I thought as I surreptitiously watched him move from student to student, suggesting this or that addition to the creamy, buttery Senegalese soup we were making. This, at least, I didn't think I could screw up too badly, and some hot soup would be lovely for my dinner the next couple of nights. These four classes we'd spent together, even in this commercial kitchen and surrounded by other students, with Edgar's perfectly composed and professional demeanor, was the closest thing to domesticity we'd ever shared.

In fact, I realized, *La Table* was the only building we'd ever been in together. All our strange communion belonged to the night and the streets.

I had a moment of panic when we came to my apartment

steps later that night, a sudden terror this was the end. Perhaps what I imagined we had was only some elaborate game Edgar liked to play. Perhaps he picked a particularly gullible student to toy with every time the restaurant offered these classes. Perhaps the entire affair was only a sop to his ego that allowed him the game while never actually committing him to betraying his wife.

I thought of those jade eyes, the eerie connection that had crackled between us. Perhaps the game, in fact, was hers.

Too many fears to put into words, too much vulnerability to put on display. All I could muster was a weak, "Tomorrow?"

Edgar smiled as he lifted my chin and kissed both my eyebrows. "Tomorrow."

All my doubts vanished. He had such power over me. I wonder, sometimes, how long our chaste courtship would have lasted had fate not intervened. Was the unwinding already set in stone? Did he know, even then, Octavia's costume was wearing thin? Or might he have persuaded me to wait not only months but years?

We didn't know it at that moment, but the horror story of our age had already begun. We'd heard whispers of a new sickness ravaging the east, but with our typical blithe American arrogance, we assumed it would never reach us.

February 28th. The last day of our little cooking class. The first day, I learned later, the plague reached Oregon. Tiffany and I had only completed our second salsa class—no broken bones yet, only bruises and general humiliation—when we got word the instructor had fallen ill, and classes were cancelled. Another two weeks and the world was shut down.

Edgar and I exchanged phone numbers at last. Watching him with his phone felt almost surreal and disappointingly prosaic at the same time. It was some kind of proof he did, in fact, exist in the real world, not just in the space we shared. The perfectly functional device also demonstrated, I told myself, he almost certainly *isn't* a vampire, since technology tends to short out around them.

At least according to all the best vampire romance novels. Not that I had particularly strong suspicions in that regard, but it's always best to keep an open mind. However, it appeared Edgar Leyward was just a garden-variety shockingly handsome, not so temperamental, well-read master chef cheating on his wife.

Emotionally cheating on his wife, that is.

CHAPTER FIVE

We never talked about Octavia. I wonder if that is a common discretion among the unfaithful. I'd always imagined cheating partners to be continually bemoaning their unappreciated state or complaining about negligence or boredom or whatever sort of tattered nightgown their spouse wore these days. But although Edgar didn't speak of her, I was somehow certain he adored her. He never acted the part of the beleaguered or unsatisfied husband, never came to me wan and worn and in search of propping up. If anything, he was the picture of good health in every way.

And health was shortly to become our overriding national obsession.

When the pandemic had arrived in earnest and the first quarantine orders were issued, it was all rather jolly. A shocking diversion for a nation wearied by continual gaslighting and groping and grasping, from the highest levels of government to the businesses whose profit margins dictated our daily conveniences. At last, we had a real, definable problem. A problem no one could deny, something the whole world grappled with. The simplest—or only—solution was to stay home, snuggle up, play board games, do jigsaw puzzles, and consume copious amounts of television and tequila.

The brief lurid euphoria of it all quickly vanished amidst images of stacked coffins, crowded hospital hallways, and funerals attended only by the dead and their priest. All around the world, people were suffering alone, dying alone, and being buried alone.

We watched desperate family members holding up signs outside hospital windows in the hopes the ill would see them. We listened to wheezing deathbed goodbyes over telephones featured as nightly news stories. We watched as the wealthy and the powerful died— not as easily or as often as the poor, but the fact they were at all subjected to our same peril was a new and strange reality.

And how wrong we were to think this crisis would unite us against a common enemy. Almost as soon as we learned how to pronounce the name of the virus, we politicized it. Half the country claimed there was no risk at all in getting sick and refused to take the simplest precautions, and both sides rapidly decamped to positions behind their favorite celebrity billionaires. Throughout every tier of society, people were exhausted, angry, and increasingly cynical. Above all, we were afraid. Those most frightened of all were the ones closing their eyes against the monster and insisting they couldn't be killed as long as they refused to acknowledge its reality.

I was one of the few still working. The library had closed, of course, but we still took book orders online. I would roam the stacks in my mask and gloves and fill a bag with books, and when the patrons came by to pick them up, we used the library foyer like an airlock. They would wave through the glass and gratefully scrunch their eyes at me over their masks, and I would feel more alone than ever.

I almost think it would have been easier if I'd been furloughed like Evan and the rest of my coworkers. I could have joined *Tiger King* watch parties on social media or held Zoom meetings over martinis and somehow muddled through the communal trauma as if it were indeed communal. As it was, I felt doubly isolated. The library that had been my haven for so long assumed the affect of some lonely, haunted dungeon—long forgotten and buried under the sea. The hum of the ventilation system and the cocooning of the false light thoroughly divided me from the world outside. I tried to make merry with my masks, stitching up ghoulish faces or festooning them with black and red lace, but without Evan to mock my macabre, it felt pointless.

I told myself I should be grateful I had a job, and more grateful still I wasn't working in a grocery store or a pharmacy, where the exhausted staff were continually battered with all their customers' stress, anxiety, fear, and resentment on top of the constant risk of exposure. Grateful I wasn't sick. I was like a mad little lab rat, wildly scurrying from loneliness to fear to guilt to shame and back to loneliness again.

Texting Evan was weirdly awkward. We both felt out-of-place and a little insecure about how our new realities related to each other: he was staying home and making more money on unemployment than he had while working in the library, whereas I, at least, had some sense of purpose, some tangible list of accomplishments I could still use to justify my existence in a capitalist society. We were both miserable, but our miseries couldn't talk to one another.

I got a couple of messages from Tiffany, too, early on, but we hadn't had the most meaningful friendship before quarantine. So, when the friendship began to struggle and stumble toward what seemed an inevitable death, we let it go. I loved my parents, but we didn't have much in common. I'd call them now and then, of course. Dad would rumble out the latest headlines he was watching on TV, while Mom would tell me all the ways I could possibly die or fall into despair or—as she always seemed to think was my most likely fate—get sex-trafficked. I'd hoped at some point she'd realize I was past the prime marketable age on that score, but it didn't seem to be happening. So, those calls were more chore than comfort.

As for Edgar ... the distance was gutting.

This wasn't the romantic yearning penned by the writers of Regency romances or those luridly illustrated books whose covers featured bodybuilding Highland chiefs dressed in nothing but kilts. This was a blood-sickness. If I could have driven him from my thoughts, I would have, so wretched and ragged I felt with the constant *pluck, pluck, pluck* of his absence on my consciousness. He was the first thing I thought of when I woke up. My brain conjured endless contrived conversations between us as I roamed the deserted stacks at work. I dreamed of him and woke, sweating, consumed with a strange, excited anxiety, staring into the darkness and unable to retrieve any details of his phantasm.

By the end of the second week, I realized I must have secretly hoped time and distance would prove some antidote to his wonderful poison, that space would clear my vision, show me all we were was crass and common and selfish and fleeting. Hoped I'd save myself from myself before it could go too far. While he could still maintain some pretense of honesty. Hoped all the peacock feathers and stardust would show themselves only false hope and detritus in the end, cheap and pathetic and completely beneath me.

Instead, day and night, each cell in my body tended toward an intersection that hourly grew farther away. We'd exchanged numbers, true, in some unspoken nod toward a potential apocalypse we both wanted to pretend was impossible. A mistress—no, that's not right. As much as my inner melodrama-mama craved the title, I knew I hadn't earned it. I wasn't even an illicit lover. Just an unacknowledged friend. Regardless, an unacknowledged friend can't send texts. Can't cling for survival in the awful isolation of quarantine to another woman's husband.

You might assume that didn't matter to me, that I wouldn't have attached myself so hopelessly to him if it had, but it did matter, more than I can express. Even now, after all this time, I sometimes dream of those jade eyes bidding me goodbye. I wake up, breathless, choking, my throat full of aquamarine waters and my fingers dripping with seaweed. I think: *I nearly drowned there*, and something in me is disappointed I survived when I might have been subsumed by her. Other days, I imagine I see her eyes flashing at me beneath my lashes in the mirror, and I wonder which of us truly made it to the surface in the end.

So no texts. No little messages of hope and cheer and grim,

dark-hearted urgency that somehow, through all the madness, we must survive. No invisible threads of connection spun together by words. No droplets of his voice falling into my consciousness. No bridges from hour to hour through the day.

But sometimes, late at night or early in the morning, depending on how you look at it, he would call. I would lie on my side, with the blanket pulled over my head, and close my eyes while his voice became my entire universe. I tried to listen to the exactitude of the words, I did, but as often I became lost in the music of the low, rumbling symphony of his tongue tangling with the streets and the rain and the in-between.

He would slip out sometimes and pace the sidewalk in front of his house after Octavia fell asleep. He took up pipe-smoking—his quarantine hobby, he called it—to further his excuse in case of any suspicion. I pictured him, in his long foglifter and his leather flat cap, with a curved pipe dangling from his wide lips. Somehow, he'd gone from sexy chef to Scottish professor. I couldn't convince myself that detracted from his appeal.

Even that pitiful contact only lasted a few days. Octavia wasn't feeling well, he told me one night. I hardly breathed, startled by the mention of her name, as if it had summoned her between us. I hope she feels better soon, I finally mumbled, unsure if it were some sacrilege for me to soil her name with my lips. I kept my gaze fixed on his face, convinced if my eyes once slipped into the shadow beneath his arm, I would see her standing there, her eyes burning into me like two will-o'-the-wisps, taunting me onto unsafe ground.

And then he was gone.

Two whole weeks passed without a word. I could have used the time to get over him, I suppose. Already I knew that could not happen. My fatalism was a stranger to me, but I could do little better than dress and name it and hope to be stronger than it in the end. I found myself possessed of the strangest detachment. Almost as if I were trailing along beside my own body, only scarcely sensing what afflictions of passion and obsession consumed the spirit, animated it. My life was rapidly becoming a novel I was reading instead of writing.

Maybe Edgar was only nursing his sick wife, maybe he was suffering an acute attack of conscience and shunning me altogether, maybe he would call tomorrow, or tomorrow, or tomorrow. It did not matter. I would live in want of him, always.

I wasn't some silly dime novel heroine. Was I? A woman has more needs than the wind in her hair and a pair of brooding eyes to dream about. I'd find some other diversion. I'd even find a lover, a friend, someone to spend my remaining years with. But this piece of me, this piece shaped like library stacks and cooking classes and rainy sidewalks and snowy embraces and loneliness—this piece would keep its edges, this piece would only ever fit Edgar Leyward. I could only hope the other pieces still formed something like a whole person.

And then he called.

CHAPTER SIX

"**S**igrun."

I froze, standing on the wheely steps I used to reach the top shelves at the library. I'd answered my phone without even glancing at the display, more focused on the precarious stack of books crookedly piled in my other arm.

Edgar.

My name was a prayer on his lips, a prayer I already somehow knew I couldn't answer.

"Edgar?"

"Sigrun." Then came the awful choking silence peculiar to the mourner, who tries and tries to speak without weeping but cannot. "Sigrun."

I sank onto the steps, allowing the books to gently cascade out of my arms into a haphazard heap on the floor.

In my mind's eye I saw the pale blue-gray gleam of a dolphin's glistening curve leaping through turquoise waters, lit by a scarlet and tangerine sunset. A cliff loomed in the distance, black and menacing, and my mind skittered away from its brink.

Translucent jade.

"Sigrun," he tried again. I don't know, even now, how many times he tried. Finally, the awful truth came through.

"Octavia is gone."

My stomach caverned away from me, a sinkhole of incomprehension. Such a beautiful, bright, mysterious creature—dead? Decaying? Undone? How could that be true?

Once the worst was plainly said, his words came in a torrent. Weaker than he knew. Just terribly tired, they'd both thought. Just needed to sleep, to rest. Wrapped in her husband's arms, sweating against his chest. A trip to the ER, just to bring down the fever, he'd thought, but they learned too late she'd been starving for air. A gurney, taking her away. Her frightened eyes. Ventilator. A nurse had held the phone for her. She hadn't said a word at the end. Couldn't, with the tube in her throat. But Edgar had. He'd poured his soul out across a little metal rectangle held up by a stranger to his dying wife's ear. And then she'd gone quiet, and the machines had gone loud.

"Sigrun," he prayed again.

But I was no god. I clutched my phone and cried as if my heart would break.

"Edgar," I finally managed. "Will—will there be a funeral?"

It wasn't as if I hadn't been watching the news. What else was there to do after I dragged myself home? Every day a new catastrophe or new national embarrassment dominated the headlines. I'd developed an actual horror of missing a story. With my luck, I'd sign off just as they were announcing the rise of Arawn's army of the undead or some new plague of flesh-eating Miller moths. Unhealthy, I know, but the compulsion was very real.

At any rate, I knew no one was holding funerals right now. From what I could glean, the Catholics and the Jews could at least get a priest to consign the dead to the afterlife. Bleakly, I wondered if imams performed similar services. There was so much I didn't know, I thought, before forcing myself to refocus.

Grief, most mutual of human feelings, our first friend and our final companion, had been forced into solitary confinement. Funerals, American-Protestant style, are arguably the unhealthiest acknowledgment of loss, but we'd lost even those. No wakes. No celebrations. No shared stories and pints and tears. Every one of us was locked away, locked away from each other, locked away from mortality even as we waited in terror for its arrival on our doorstep. That controversial grace of a last kiss, a last confession, a last goodbye had been stolen from us. We were forced to bear the unbearable. Even animals comfort one another after a loss. Even those like me, who staunchly clung to their identities as introverts or just general outsiders, learned too well and too late we were herd animals after all. And without our herd to protect us, succor us, we were all suffering from a wasting disease.

It wasn't that we didn't try. We did. Social media exploded. Cheery signs with random messages of encouragement appeared on lawns. People put out Christmas lights early or decorated their windows. Stamps and stationery made a comeback. But those moments when the only thing you needed in the world was a hug from your mom or your friend or your sister—those moments went unanswered.

"No funeral," Edgar managed. "I—I'm not sure where I'm burying her yet."

Palpable agony reached me through the phone. I didn't know how he was going to get through the next few days. I'd never had to be the adult for death, never had to organize a burial. There must be so many calls to place, decisions to make, at a time when the brain had no resources left for decisions. And Edgar would have to do it alone, with no one to stand beside him, hold his hand, take notes, decide what color satin and what the stone should read. Which of her lovely dresses Octavia should wear for her long sleep under the dirt.

"I'm so sorry, Edgar. I don't know what to say. Is there anything I can do? Calls I can make for you?" Wildly inappropriate, I know, for the other woman to help with the wife's funeral, but who else was there?

For half a beat it occurred to me I didn't know the answer to that question. I knew about Edgar's family: his parents down in southern California, a brother in Minnesota. Travel into Oregon was restricted because of the virus, but perhaps Octavia's family were nearby.

I decided against asking.

"I don't think so." He sounded unutterably weary. "I don't think I can talk anymore. I just needed—I needed to hear your voice."

He hung up without saying goodbye.

I sat there on the floor a long time, stacking and unstacking and restacking the books I had collected. It's strange, really. Death is the most normal and ubiquitous thing in the whole world. Who even knows how many little insect lives we snuff out on our way to work? How many mice and butterflies and praying mantis and daddy-longlegs breathe their last while we sleep in our beds? I dare say only sociopaths have never cried their eyes out over the loss of a beloved pet. And as for people—we live in constant, unfailing awareness of it. Yet, every time it arrives, it dresses up as a surprise, an impossibility, something completely contrary to the rules of nature.

And it did seem impossible. I kept picturing Octavia on the one night I had seen her in Edgar's class. How could such a powerful, vibrant creature be gone? How did she go from lying in her husband's arms one night to dying on a machine days later? Our paths had intersected so briefly, but surely the shimmering darkness pulsing behind those green eyes could not be banished by something as mundane as a string of viral particles. Even now, my fancy insisted her force vibrated in the air beside me: waiting, baleful, malignant. Resentful, my shell still housed me while hers had rejected her.

I attempted an awkward titter as if laughing at my silly delusions would dispel my discomfort, but the sound of my own voice only, oddly, irritated me.

Would it have mattered if Edgar had been in the room beside her? Would his love have been strong enough to anchor her to the earth even when her body thought itself too weak?

I knew, logically, it was a nonsensical question. People died in the presence of their loved ones all the time. But it has always been a difficult reality for me to accept. That in one moment, you have their warm hand in yours, you are gazing right into the light of their eyes, you are begging them to stay, yet still they slip away? The hand goes cold, and those eyes go dark and frosted with otherness. All the heart strings you had so tightly knotted simply snap.

How can that be possible? Be real?

I saw again Edgar sweeping Octavia up in his ridiculously theatrical embrace, heard her laughter. I thought of him clutching his phone, alone in his car in the hospital parking lot, as near to her as he could get, trying and failing to pour enough strength and will and magic into his voice to keep her here.

How could Octavia be gone? Impossible things happen all the time.

CHAPTER SEVEN

Two days later, I was parked outside the Forest Glen cemetery. The gates to the graveyard were closed, but I had seen Edgar's car in the funeral home lot. I didn't want to cause any trouble by illegally crashing a quarantine burial. On the other hand, I wasn't about to let Edgar bury his wife completely alone. I wouldn't ask a stranger to endure that. Hells bells, I wouldn't let an enemy go through that alone.

Spring was blustering her way in, but the early morning was still quite chilly with frost clinging to the edges of pale green leaves boldly unfurling from their winter sleep. The library wouldn't be open for at least another hour. I figured Edgar had scheduled the burial so early so he wouldn't have to sit around in his lonely house and wait for the clock hands to tell him it was time to go put his wife in the ground. I wondered if he'd slept at all last night.

I had my answer when he finally emerged. Fear leaped into my throat at the sight of him. He looked like a wasted ghoul dressed up in the clothes of the living. His normally dusky face wasn't just pale: it was practically gray. His clothes hung on his big frame, and I don't think he'd brushed his hair. His eyes stared and stared like some orbs that looked only on hell, and he didn't even notice me as he walked over to his car and tried fruitlessly to get the door handle to work.

I got out of the car and waved my arm, and was surprised when my action caught his eye, as shattered as he seemed.

"Edgar," was all I could manage. What more could I say?

He leaned his arms on the roof of his car as if he barely had the strength left to stand and simply gazed at me. I was no longer sure why I'd come, what I'd thought to offer. Was this a terrible mistake? Was he angry or offended I'd have the gall to show up here?

I didn't care. It wasn't about me. His ache, his emptiness, opened before me like a black hole into which all my being could only stream. Some last gasp of self was strung out on the event horizon, shredded into ever-more translucent strands of light, watching helplessly as he drew me closer into his terrible darkness. How could I resist? Why would I want to? I couldn't remember a single reason.

"It's so cold," he finally said, sounding more broken than I could have ever imagined. I knew he was thinking of Octavia lying alone in the dark, in the cold. Never again to be consoled, never again to be warmed.

A half-dozen platitudes rose to my lips, but I swallowed them all. None of them were true. Or they were all true, but they didn't matter. Not one of them could undo this loss or ease this pain. I just stood there in the shelter of my open car door, rubbing one lace beribboned calf against the other, prompted as much by nervousness as by chill.

"I should be better at this by now," he said.

That struck me as both odd and generally untrue.

He shook his head bleakly. "There's no way through at all," he said. "This is here. This is it. This is the place I occupy now. The place she isn't. I try to escape, but I keep coming back to it, again and again."

What kind of person gets good at goodbye? I demurred. "I don't think there's a right way through this." He was being way too hard on himself. It wasn't as if grief was a skill we practiced, after all. "Give yourself time."

He laughed harshly, and the sound was more frightening than the despair in his eyes. "Oh, time. It does taunt me."

He wasn't making much sense, but then, I didn't figure exhausted, grief-stricken people usually did. One more reason why we need helpers when we are mourning. Someone to put us to bed, someone to get us out of bed, someone to hand us plates and take glasses out of our hands and make sure we don't wander off any cliffs before our senses return. But that year—that year, too many people didn't have helpers. Somehow or another, I was determined Edgar would have me.

He sort of shook himself then, and finally managed to operate the door handle. "I'd better let you get to work," he said distantly. "Goodbye, Sigrun."

Those two words possessed a terrible finality as if he'd come to some sort of decision and I stood on the outside of it. Perhaps he had. But at any rate, he couldn't stick to it. A few hours later, a text came through. The first text, in fact, I'd ever gotten from him.

Sigrun. Thank you for being there. Can you come over tonight?

As if I could tell him no. As if I'd ever want to.

I went home after work and threw together a quick dish of smothered burritos I could toss in the oven once I got to his house. He didn't look like he'd been eating much. Even if he hadn't the appetite tonight, Mexican food only gets better with time. I'd had to ask him for his address. I'd never been there before, of course. Pulling into the back alley drive, I couldn't help a shiver of foreboding. I was ninety-five percent sure I believed in ghosts, and it was hard to fathom Octavia accepting my trespass here.

Unsurprisingly, their home was lovely. Far more grown-up than my studio apartment with its horror-movie posters and random swaths of red and gray lace and black velvet on the walls. Their house managed to feel warm and welcoming in spite of its obvious glamour, probably owing to all the thickly carved wooden moldings of its Craftsman-style architecture. I'd been right, my brain noted absently, to think of Octavia as Zelda. Stained glass and Art Deco paintings added to a general sense of grace and slightly shabby glitz. I felt out-of-place in my mid-calf black velvet dress and its thigh-high split, the ribboned fishnets, and requisite boots. Those, at least,

I slipped off in the entryway.

He hadn't spoken when he opened the door, but his face broke in a way I took as a welcome. I padded past him as if I knew where I was going and followed my instincts to the kitchen.

As I should have expected, the room was a marvel. Gleaming dark walnut cabinets with polished chrome hardware surrounded a huge black marble-topped island. I could only imagine what sort of magical cooking implements and esoteric ingredients lay hidden in the cabinets and what appeared to be not one but two pantries. I placed my glass dish heaped with meat and veggies and tortillas and cheese and canned green chili sauce in the oven and turned the temperature way up.

"You're probably not hungry now," I acknowledged to the ghost of Edgar who had meekly followed me into his kitchen, "but hopefully the smell will tempt you. Everyone loves the smell of hot peppers and melted cheese."

Somehow, he actually smiled then. "Brave girl," he said hollowly, "cooking for a professional chef."

His smile widened at my sudden look of horror. "I hadn't even thought about it," I confessed. "But I think you already know from class that my kitchen skills are—ahem. Rudimentary. No! Utilitarian."

"I'm grateful," he said, his face falling back into its cavernous lines as if the brief lift had taken all his strength. I followed him back into the living room, perched beside him on the very edge of the buttery-soft tobacco leather couch as if I were some weird little church lady "paying a call."

We sat there in silence for a long while. In the companionable quietude, an otherness shifted silkily under my skin. The shapes of the furniture, the shadows cast on the walls, no longer held the allure of the strange but took on the reassurance of the familiar. I imagined a dark hand pushed me back against the cushions, urging me to ease. I watched my hand move unhesitatingly to rest on his broad thigh as if it belonged to someone else, someone bolder than me. He covered my fingers with the palm of his hand as he released a deep, shuddering sigh.

"I have to tell you something," he said at last, his voice so low I caught my breath to listen.

"I'm listening," I said.

"This isn't the first time this has happened," he said. He seemed to be gathering his thoughts, and every word took incredible effort, so I waited without questioning as he stumbled through more of his story than I had ever guessed at.

Edgar had been a widower once before, but even that had not been his first experience with loss. Before he'd dropped out of college to attend culinary school, he'd been madly in love with a young chemical engineering student named Devlin. Theirs had been a wild, fiery match, conflagrated on their first encounter. From the moment he'd met her, he'd never wanted anyone else. She was his soulmate, his forever.

She was brilliant and unpredictable and passionate and reckless. Reckless was a high-risk factor for someone who'd been born with Type I diabetes. Edgar hadn't really known much about the disease at the time—she'd hidden it from him as much as she could, glossing over what she couldn't. They'd gone on a camping trip together, followed up a decadent night of alcohol and sex with a hard morning hike in the Idaho wilderness. When she'd collapsed, Edgar had no idea what to do. And maybe he couldn't have done anything. Regardless, long before Search-and-Rescue arrived, she was catatonic, and she died before they got her to the hospital.

Her death had been the real reason Edgar had left the university. His whole universe shifted when he lost Devlin. He'd always loved cooking, loved the creative aspect of it, but mostly the time spent in the kitchen was a practiced diversion, a trick to play on his brain to convince it to keep functioning. And eventually, cooking became an end to itself, an honest-to-God passion licked from the flames of hell and death.

His second real restaurant gig was where he met his first wife. I had a hard time picturing my Edgar, so exacting and dramatic, obediently following recipe cards in a PF Chang's, but apparently it had actually happened. Brigitte had been the restaurant manager.

Ah, I thought, *here we have the origins of the French-Asian fusion he so adores.*

He'd been reluctant, he told me, to let her in, but she'd insisted. She'd hounded and courted him, not the other way around. I mused privately on the sexual harassment implications, but he clearly hadn't been bothered. His reluctance had stemmed solely from the agony of losing Devlin that still defined his entire world. He hadn't wanted to risk his heart a second time.

But Brigitte had won him over. They'd married, moved to Oregon together, started their restaurant. She was the books person, he was the creative, and together they opened one of Portland's most successful boutique restaurants. There'd been magazine articles and morning show debuts. They'd been perfectly in sync, right up until her breast cancer diagnosis.

Her mother, her aunt, and her grandmother had all died of breast cancer. She had the gene, so she'd gone in to have a full mastectomy when she was only twenty. I found it oddly touching Edgar never mentioned that to me when describing her and their sweet short love, only divulging it in his bitterness how it hadn't helped. She'd died anyway, a long slow death but still not slow enough. Their restaurant had gone belly-up almost without him noticing. He'd liquidated everything he could and stayed home with her until the end.

He'd actually met Octavia before Brigitte died. She'd been one of the home nurses assigned to them once they went into hospice care. I had a hard time picturing that. The lovely, ethereal Octavia changing bedpans and sopping up vomit, sweating as she lifted patients into wheelchairs and bath chairs and beds? But she had done exactly that.

An uncomfortable thought intruded. What if Edgar had simply determined never to be alone again after Devlin? What if he'd groomed Octavia to step into Brigitte's position as soon as she was gone? Had he groomed me, too?

I flushed with the foolishness of it all. How patently ridiculous. There was no way he could have known Octavia would contract this dreaded virus when he and I had met. Not to mention how deeply he'd loved her. The last thing he'd been imagining was that she'd be taken like she had been.

Right?

Of course, that was right. We hadn't so much as heard about the virus when we'd met—or if we had, it was only as some strange flu attacking people half a world away. We certainly hadn't guessed it would compound, killing hundreds of thousands of us with impunity while the rest of the world watched in horror while in quarantine.

Still, I felt uncomfortable to share this eerie juxtaposition with Octavia, how we'd both arrived before the other had fully exited. Edgar, though, insisted he'd hardly even noticed Octavia during Brigitte's last days. It had only been when they'd run into each other by chance in some Portland wine bar, where he'd been drowning his sorrows and she'd been toasting hers, that they'd made a real connection.

When he'd taken the job offer from *La Table* three months later, Octavia had come with him. A real whirlwind, I couldn't help thinking, especially for a grieving husband. But some people do find each other like that. She'd taken a position with hospice in Forest Glen as an administrator instead of a nurse, which was so much easier for me to picture. I could imagine, though, how her newly regular hours combined with a chef's evening schedule would create an unintended rift. Not that Edgar had ever seemed unhappy with Octavia. He'd simply, in some inexplicable way, drew me in without pushing her out.

Now, though, he was widowed a second time, bereaved a third. And barely past thirty. What terrible luck.

Have I mentioned my go-to trauma response is humor? To be honest, I haven't experienced any real trauma in my life, besides the deaths of my two cats and a dog. I think that's part of my fascination with horror. My best friend in elementary school was a foster kid. My high school boyfriend lost his best friend to a hit-and-run when we were seventeen. Both sets of my grandparents were dead by the time I was eight. I've witnessed enough trauma without ever experiencing it first-hand to know how it lurks on every corner. I live in terror of its arrival, so I practice, practice, practice, all the time.

As if any practice could mute the voice of loss when it keens.

Still, I tried. I didn't know what else to do. But when the awful moment did arrive—when death burst, full-grown, from my fingertips, I was so terribly, terribly unprepared.

That's later, though. Back to Edgar and my inappropriate humor.

"I can't deny it puts a damper on things, learning you're a black widower."

The words fell flat, even to my own ears.

CHAPTER EIGHT

It's hard to describe how completely the pandemic altered our lives. Every plan we'd made, every expectation we'd had, wasn't simply delayed: it was lost. The machines of society threw spinners, shattered gears, ground to a halt. We kept trying to repair them, but it was like rebuilding the towers of a sandcastle as the tide came in. Relationships, strained mercilessly by isolation and enforced company, changed irrevocably, some for better, some for worse. All our definitions were rewritten: church, school, family, friends, work, communication, acceptable, unacceptable. We became more tolerant than we ever would have imagined in some ways and lost patience entirely in others. We re-examined our laws, our beliefs, our standards. The comfortable became rebels, revolutionaries lost themselves in a haze of drugs and alcohol, and titans fell like statues.

Perhaps that will help explain how Edgar and I fell so completely into each other. He was terribly lost in those early days. I feared to leave him alone. It wasn't that I thought he would hurt himself, exactly. He didn't rage and threaten and carry on. It was the way he sat, like a scarecrow whose stuffing had been pulled out, with eyes like black stitched crosses staring into emptiness. I found him more frightening still when he did rouse, pulling me onto his lap and sinking his hands deep into my hair, kissing me eyes open as if he would search me inside out.

My body, which he had held so sacrosanct until now, became the only opium for his pain. Some evenings we hardly spoke a word, only slaked our strange loneliness with pleasure. Nothing alleviates grief. No human touch can even reach it. And it is an awful thing to watch someone twisting and writhing in its flames that burn and burn and never consume. So, to the wound I could not heal I added comfort and solace and mindless, mad indulgences to wear out his body and allow his mind to sleep. We were like insects following each other through the dark, our questing hands constantly reassuring ourselves of the other's presence.

The restaurant was closed. Some restaurants had been able to shift to a pick-up menu and were struggling along at a reduced schedule and staff, but *La Table*'s specialty items and gourmet menu made that impossible. Edgar was still maintaining the restaurant's blog and social media feeds, but I wasn't sure how long *La Table* could survive before the owner had to make some decisions about the future of his career and his business. We didn't discuss finances, but Edgar didn't seem worried.

Aside from our first night of burritos, Edgar did all the cooking. I think the ritual was soothing to him, something creative and sustaining for his hands and mind to focus on. I came over every night after dashing home from work for a quick shower and often stayed until morning. Our time together was an unvoiced assumption we both made.

Three weeks after Octavia's death, Edgar glanced up at me over the salmon he was seasoning. "You should just move in," he said, waving vaguely at the overnight bag in my right hand.

I hardly even surprised myself when I simply nodded and agreed that would be best. The next day, I gave my landlord notice. My lease wouldn't be up for two months yet, but the cushion period just gave me more time to move. Not that my few belongings would amount to more than two or three carloads. Not that much, even, if I didn't take my furniture. It's not as if my horror-punk sensibilities matched Edgar's sophisticated décor. I assured my wax-splattered candlesticks and coffin-styled coffee table their exile wasn't permanent, though I couldn't imagine when I'd unbox them. I forced down the unease pounding on my spine, shouting for me to keep a tighter grip on my identity.

I'm growing as a person, I whispered. I'm not losing myself.

I should have felt like an outsider, like I was invading another woman's house, but I didn't. Even in Edgar and Octavia's room, with its massive burgundy-and-gold draped sleigh bed and the walls hung with Eduard Gordeev prints, I felt no uneasiness. Anchored deep in my heart was an immoveable conviction: Edgar was home to me. Wherever he was, I belonged.

He had as few misgivings as I did. He didn't so much as blink when his austere bathroom counter became littered with cosmetics and hair accessories and a ghoulish silver candelabra dripping with black candles. One day I came home and found he'd moved all Octavia's elegant and colorful wardrobe into the spare bedroom's closet and chest-of-drawers, leaving space open for my drear and stark clothes instead. One night I laughingly suggested he needed a mirror hung on the stamped-tin ceiling over the bed, and a week later a huge ornate mirror arrived in the mail. The ostentatious thing had cost nearly as much to ship as it was worth.

The world outside grew more macabre daily, more unfamiliar. Body counts mounted, not only in our own country but around the world. Here and there the virus would be stamped out, only to roar back to life weeks later. Was this what it had felt like in the opening days and months of the Dark Ages? Had they—like us—foolishly imagined renewal was inevitable, unaware they were about to plunge into hundreds of years of cold and dark and famine and disease and lose thousands of years' worth of knowledge? Not only was the virus our enemy now, but time itself and in its train, the specters of poverty and chaos and despair.

So how could we not turn more and more into each other? Outsiders might have found us opposites, but in Edgar's company, I had never felt more myself. Inside those walls, all our boundaries became gates. I found myself watching the clock at work as I never had, impatient to be back under his gaze and in his arms. And he seemed as hungry for my company as I was for his.

It was a peculiarity of his house that none of the walls or bookshelves or tabletops held a single personal photo. Instead, his home was adorned with small sculptures and artifacts and hung with works of art. In the small front room with the wide window seat that functioned as a library and office, I found three fat photobooks, the sort you make online with digital photos that are perfect-bound and shipped to you. On their spines, I traced their titles: *Devlin, Brigitte, Octavia.*

My stomach lurched a bit, a mixture of anticipation and dread. Something dark crawled around uncomfortably under my skin to see Octavia's name emblazoned there already. I told myself it wasn't so strange. After all, Edgar was here alone for hours while I was at the library. People were allowed to go on neighborhood walks or to the grocery store or the pharmacy, but that was all. No sitting at a corner café or catching a movie or visiting a neighborhood bar. The city had even closed the parks. So it wasn't as if Edgar hadn't had plenty of time to create this book of legacy.

Still, when I pictured Edgar sitting alone at his computer while I scavenged library books for my patrons, clicking through photo after photo of his dead wives and girlfriend and painstakingly sorting them into a glossy-covered book, goosebumps swelled on my bare arms. Simple envy, I told myself sternly. What living woman could resist a little jealousy of the lovely and ephemeral Octavia?

And it was understandably morbid to see their names stacked on his shelves like so many toe tags. These books were all that remained of three women Edgar had loved so deeply, all still standing testament to the infinite and infinitesimally small ripples their lives had made in the pool that was the universe. I felt suddenly anxious I had no book of my own.

What if I got hit by a bus tomorrow? Well, not a bus. The buses weren't running these days. But a car. Or a semi. What if I had an aneurysm, just blinked out with no warning at all? What if, in spite of all the care we took, the virus took me just as it had taken Octavia?

I knew Edgar did have a handful of photos of me. He always had a camera close by, mostly for his food blog, but occasionally he'd decide I looked particularly inspiring and snap a shot. He loved my macabre and fanciful style, and I tell you without a shred of boasting that my makeup is always elaborate and flawless. This does require an inordinate amount of bathroom mirror time, but I enjoy it. It calms me to put myself together every day like that. With my false eyelashes and porcelain cheeks and marron-black lipstick, I feel pretty near unassailable.

So, it's been disconcerting, to say the least, to look in the mirror some days and find I must have been experimenting with Octavia's high-dollar cosmetics that I found in a bottom drawer. Colors and shades I'd eschewed in the past were delicately painted and contoured over my bones like I was some department store model. I kind of remembered pulling them out and opening the glossy lids, but for the life of me, I couldn't imagine why I'd adopt such demure and retiring hues. Maybe it was the sheer indulgence of the brands and the silky soft powders and liquids. I'd even been trying to draw out the green in my hazel eyes instead of ringing them in black and lavender. At one point, I found myself examining my ebony locks and considering adding a streak or two of white to my black hair, just to lighten the effect a little. Madness, right? The one consolation I had to offer myself for such weirdly wallflower behavior was that, at least, the macabre practice of using a dead woman's makeup was entirely on-brand for me. BUT I digress.

All that said, we hadn't had many photogenic memories together. No date nights out or—thank goodness—camping trips or museum jaunts. Now that we lived together, even our midnight walks had been abridged. He still stepped out from time to time, with the silly pipe he'd adopted. I'd watch him from the window for a few minutes sometimes, enjoying his dapper silhouette strolling off into the shadows like some moody English detective. Now that I no longer lived for stolen minutes, though, I preferred luxuriating in our satiny king-size sheets to tromping what as often as not were rainy streets.

How thin a little space all my time with Edgar would occupy on this shelf, I thought. Instead of a book, he could make a brochure.

Just then I heard the shower door pop open and shot guiltily out of the study. I landed on the living room couch in a swirl of black taffeta, snatched up the remote, and nonchalantly reviewed the evening's offerings. I didn't know why I did that. Edgar behaved as if he had no secrets from me, and he answered every question I asked without hesitation. His most likely reaction on finding me looking at his photo books would be to describe the setting or the story behind whatever photo was on the open page. Still, I said nothing about my find when he walked into the living room.

I maintained my discretion for all of fifteen minutes before guilt overwhelmed me, and I confessed my snooping in a rush of jumbled words.

CHAPTER NINE

He forgave me, of course.

I was awkward and anxious, and full-bore Sigrun on every front, and still he forgave me.

It was the strangest and most difficult of times, and the only way to survive was to give each other grace. To give each other grace and to hold on with all the strength we had to any bits we could reach.

So that's what we did.

And six weeks later we were married, in masks, with some magazine-ad minister Edgar found on Craigslist.

I know what you're thinking. How could you not? I thought the same thing about Edgar and Octavia after Brigitte died, and they at least had the decorum to wait three months.

But as Edgar had learned long ago, and the nightly news wouldn't let me forget, life was perilously short. Even when people didn't die, they dissolved, disintegrating into vanishing grains of their own intentions and desires. The earth itself was intent on redefining herself without regard to our survival, fighting back from our incursions in the myriad ways she knew how: ice-faces collapsing, seas rising, forests burning.

We could have simply kept living together without the bond of a ring, but when everything else was indefinite, we craved something sure. And there was more to it than that. Locked inside Edgar were pieces of myself I'd been searching for all my life. Our lovemaking was a desperate, starved affair as if it weren't enough to wrap ourselves in each other's arms: I needed to be in his bones, needed his blood rushing to my heart.

People deride codependency as if it were a bad thing. As if there were some flaw in finding your perfect peace in someone else, someone who found their own peace in you. Even C.S. Lewis said something about not allowing your happiness to depend on something you might lose.

What an exceptionally nonsensical thing to say. Everything in the human experience is transient. Everything will be lost in the end. I say we should be reckless with our love and our happiness, taking it wherever we can find it for as long as we can because it will all be snatched out of our fingers eventually. And in my experience, the people who mock codependency as some sort of mental illness are either alone or with someone who can't possibly fulfill them, someone they know deep down can't be relied on for more than convenience.

Mundane love is for mundane people. I've never aspired to that.

And it wasn't as though Edgar's grief over Octavia was somehow abridged by his love for me. Sometimes, I would find him sitting slumped on the edge of the tub as the water ran, shoulders shaking in silent sobs. I would help him out of his clothes like he was a child, pour Octavia's jasmine salts into the water, gently scrub his body with the soaps I knew smelled like her, and comfort him with my body until he slept a worn and dreamless sleep.

I could tell when he was thinking about her in the kitchen. He would pause sometimes, and his fingers would go to his lips, and I knew he still felt her kiss. At night when we read in bed, his pages would stop turning, and when I looked over, his eyes would be staring at the shadows at the foot of our bed as if she stood there, watching us.

I didn't mind being haunted by Octavia. Following her soft footfalls up the stairs. Hearing my voice echo hers when I told Edgar goodnight. Imagining it was her scent, and not the flowers I caught on the wind in the garden. Seeing her face reflected in Edgar's eyes when he gazed down at me in the dim light of our bedroom. I would have been disturbed if he hadn't missed her, hadn't hurt and ached for her still. Only the coldest of hearts could have buried a wife and then left her soul there alone in the dark along with her body. It was a strange comfort to know if I left this life before him, too, he would keep me close in the crook of his arm, regardless of what other comforts he sought. Sometimes I even thought I was the shadow clinging there, and Octavia the corporeal lover.

And Edgar was not unmindful of the insecurity a new wife might feel. After I admitted my curiosity over his bookshelves, he gave me a box wrapped up like a wedding present. Inside were all the letters, cards, airline tickets, matchbooks, and other ephemera from his three previous loves. For someone else, that might have been a strange gift, but for me, it was perfect. He was unveiling the hidden chambers of his heart, taking back the keys from all other chatelaines and trusting me with every secret. In that box breathed all the ghosts he needed me to keep safe. How could I do other than lend them my lungs?

I had no reciprocal offering. Thirty-two-years old, and I'd never had a grand love affair before. Oh, I'd had relationships, and sometimes I even thought they might amount to the real thing, but caveats always intruded. Being a latter-day goth has its drawbacks. I've definitely attracted more than my fair share of weirdos: Twilight fanboys, wannabe vampires, Craigslist Wiccans, serial killer devotees, and gumball ghost-hunters. Even the weirdos, though, were better than the men initially infatuated with my "originality" or "quirkiness" who then began dropping hints about just when was I going to outgrow this phase.

With Edgar, I didn't suffer a moment's doubt. We explored and mapped out each other's wildernesses, not to conquer and control them but only to know them. Our fascination was as boundless as the edges of our badlands. And every day I found myself lingering longer and drawn deeper into those dark and rugged canyons, arroyos, and shadowlands, as enthralled by the horrors lurking there as by curiosity.

Which was just as well. It wasn't until Edgar presented me with his peculiar gift that I recognized another unique feature of love in the time of quarantine: I was rarely alone in our home.

I was alone in the library at work, though we were working toward a slow open schedule which would limit the number of patrons and require hourly cleaning of computer stations and counters and such. I hoped Evan would be the next employee to come back and had dropped several broad hints to that effect to the library administrator. Once I came home, though, solitude evaded me.

Until I'd experienced it, I didn't realize how much time I used to spend alone and how surreal it felt to have a home whose walls never knew me as an individual entity. It made me think about women in the pioneering days of the Oregon Trail. Generally, the sole caretakers of children, at least until the youngsters grew old enough to work a field or a mine shaft, those women never had a moment to themselves. After childbearing, their entire lives were spent in the company of one kind or another. The same must have been true across the pond as well, before the days of colonization and westward-ho. And was, no doubt, still true in less industrialized parts of the world. It occurred to me my previous surfeit of alone time was a wonderful luxury, a seldom-hailed benefit of feminism and the modern age.

Self-serving solitude might not make much of a protest sign or campaign banner, but I bet any candidate who'd guarantee it would turn out to be the sleeper victor of the women's vote.

I didn't miss it, though. If anything, the opposite were true. By the time I flipped off the library lights and locked the doors, my heart was a trapped bird in my chest, madly beating against my ribs. I'd never been the anxious sort and honestly have to fake sympathy with those who are, but this fizzing and bubbling in my veins that calmed only in Edgar's arms couldn't possibly be described as anything else.

Edgar, of course, spent many hours alone in the house without me. He seemed to be filling most of his days working on his new recipes, staging photographs for his food blog, and trying to lift the spirits of fellow out-of-work chefs around the country through his social media interactions. At first, I hated leaving him there, afraid he would sink into grief and not be able to climb back out while I was gone. But day by day he seemed stronger, and so I worried less and less.

Once I was home, we trailed each other through the house like ghosts at loose ends. He would paint my toenails for me while I worked on my fingernails. I would massage his shoulders while he pieced together the all-black jigsaw puzzle he'd bought as a nod to my general darkness. We'd eat his homemade gelato and my micro-wave popcorn and exclaim in horror over slasher films and hoarder documentaries.

I'd placed my box of letters on the nightstand on my side of the bed, but we spent so much time together, I never had a chance to pore over them. My gaze lingered on the beribboned lid every night as I slipped between the sheets with my latest lurid novel in hand. Finally, Edgar took pity on me.

"You can read them anytime, you know," he told me. "It won't trouble me."

I quirked an eyebrow at him, unconvinced. "It won't bother you if I lie here in bed with you, reading old letters from your dead lovers? Looking at the pictures they took with you?"

He'd placed the three photobooks in the box as well.

He shook his head. "It's not some painful thing you're resurrecting. It's my life. They're gone, but the memories are part of me now. You can hardly remind me of a loss I haven't forgotten. And besides—I loved them. That box is full of happiness, not sadness."

I smiled crookedly. "You're such a strange philosopher, Edgar Leyward."

Don't ask how, but right up until that moment I'd actually forgotten. Now it kicked me in the gut like a mule.

Edgar Leyward.

He was my husband, but he still carried her name.

CHAPTER TEN

O ctavia's bundle was tied up in silver tulle. How suitable, I thought. I'd only met her the once, but even then there'd been something about her that evoked the transparent waters of a shaded secret spring, the opalescent light of a cloud-shrouded full moon. I suddenly felt gauche, gaudy and awkward, with my very earthly thighs and black lace gown. I grimaced slightly but pressed on, tugging my satin robe a little more tightly around my less-than-elven stomach as I spread out Octavia's small hoard of memories on our sheets.

Beside me, Edgar turned a page, seemingly as untroubled as he'd claimed he would be. He was reading *The Autobiography of Mark Twain*, a dauntingly massive tome.

I parsed out a handful of matchbooks across my palm. What a funny bit of history, I thought. Not too many places even printed these things anymore, though I wasn't sure why. Were cigarette lighters really such an incredible advance in technology that matchbooks had been rendered entirely obsolete? I flicked open the little paper lid of one featuring a red-gowned flapper leaning on a wall beneath the words *Sissy's Speakeasy* and saw two matches had been used. Images of cobblestone alleyways and slouch-hatted men with dark dangerous eyes striding through foggy streets made me smile.

The other matchbooks all bore the names of unusual-sounding bars, too. I supposed that made sense: run-of-the-mill dive bars and corner saloons weren't likely to be printing them these days. Absently, I wondered how many mystery authors and screenwriters had bemoaned the death of the matchbook as a telling clue in narrative, like writers today bemoan the loss of the answering machine. My fingers lingered on the worn paper of one printed on shiny burgundy paper, whose embossed gold print read *Obladah Wine Bar*.

A little chill chased up my arms, and I shivered.

Edgar's warm, broad hand settled at the small of my back, though all his attention remained fixed on the book leaning against his bent knees.

This was it, the knowledge came to me in a flash. There were surely dozens of Portland wine bars where Octavia and Edgar might have discovered each other, but I felt certain this was the one where his eyes had first met her and seen more than a scrubs-decked nurse. Suddenly, the little bundle of paper and phosphorous sulfide felt less like a memento and more like a talisman that might return the bearer to its birthplace, to the spot that had forever changed its transience into time magic.

I lifted the flap and again found two matches missing. Had Edgar used to smoke cigarettes? Had they stood outside in the cool damp of bustling city streets and laughed, stared into each other eyes through thin streams of smoke? Or had Octavia used the excuse of a break to suck down two cigarettes and brace herself before returning to their table?

That was silly, I told myself. Brace herself for what?

But I knew what. Edgar was nothing if not overwhelming. He was and remains the most alive person I've ever met. Even in repose, he only paused, never rested. When his eyes met mine, they caught me, seized me, held me fast. In his arms, I felt as likely to be torn apart and devoured as seduced and slaked. It was impossible to stand near him and be unmoved. His breath, his glance, his barest touch, had a way of delving past my defenses and worrying out every secret hunger and hidden desire. I became fire, and he was the wind.

I could imagine Octavia caught in that wild chinook, her intentions rattling like storm shutters. I wouldn't have blamed her for stealing a few minutes for a nicotine bolster, however futile I knew it had been. The Octavia I had seen had abandoned all such resistance. If anything, she'd brought her own ignescence to his until they became a single firebrand rendering the rest of the world pale and cold.

I set the matchbooks aside, careful not to let my fingers shake while my insides were tightening.

A heavy paper napkin lay atop a stack of cards and letters. I knew the distinctive looping scrawl must be hers. Even on its poor canvas, it looked more like Victorian calligraphy than handwriting. It was a list of foods, labeled *Appetizers, Entrees, Desserts,* and *Digestifs.* Hastily, I looked up that last one on my phone. Somehow it struck me as a pet name for a hippo, but it turned out to be restaurant-speak for after-dinner drinks.

This must be the first menu Edgar had ever made for *La Table,* I realized. Where had they been when they'd brainstormed this together? He'd have been describing the dishes, she'd have made up the fancy names and scribbled them down. Some deli or coffee shop? The industrial-strength napkin didn't really conjure up fancy coffee drinks and crusty pastries. Maybe they'd gone to a burger joint or sat on the patio of some barbecue and dreamed up gourmet delights while sopping up grease and cheese and laughing together over plastic straws and French fries.

I stared at her bold strokes. Edgar might be overwhelming, but none of the women he had described to me could be called shrinking violets. It must take enormous strength of mind to care for the dying, I thought. Not to mention simple physical strength to wrangle bodies in and out of beds and baths. I wondered how long she'd been with Edgar before she transitioned her job from deathbeds to a desk. If the dreary morbidity of the work had driven her out or if she'd simply been biding her time, mistakenly thinking she had plenty of time to decide what she wanted to do with the rest of her life.

What is it about the immediacy of handwriting that brings the writer so presently to life? I fancied if I bent my ear near enough to the paper, I could hear her humming as she wrote, feel the little huffs of her breath on my cheek. My heart winced a little at the heedless joy and blind hope this napkin held, the certainty of a future that was already a past. Had Edgar been hired yet by *La Table*, or had they only been daydreaming of a distant when?

Beside me, Edgar lowered his heavy volume to the floor, switched off his bedside lamp, and settled onto his pillow with a sigh. His broad bare back with its corded muscles made it easier for me to lay the napkin aside and open the envelopes beneath.

Mostly, they held store-bought occasion cards: birthdays, anniversaries, Valentine's, even New Year's, which surprised me. Perhaps as survivors of so much death, they treasured each holiday more than I'd ever thought to do. These pre-printed missives had only been vehicles, though, as Octavia's large, florid hand filled every blank space. At least, it did in about half of them. Gradually her writing grew more vertical, almost impatient in its stride.

I was suddenly grateful Edgar had retreated into sleep and left me alone with Octavia's words. I felt like the most prurient of voyeurs, fully cognizant of the indefensible nature of my crimes and helpless to resist the compulsion.

And no wonder, for she was fully naked in her revelations. These were no requisite obligations grudgingly and politely fulfilled to a commitment she was determined to maintain. Equal parts dread and fascination filled me as I opened the envelope labeled *Happy 2020, Darling!*

My Treasure,

A new year flowers even as I feel my leaves curling and my bloom wilting. But I am unafraid of every season with you beside me. I know you will never leave me to crumble and drift away in the gusts of time that threaten weaker, lesser loves than ours. I wait only on your warm light, your fresh rain to renew me. No matter how drear the drought, I will always return.

Yours eternally, Kitten.

Nerveless, I dropped the card into my lap. *Kitten?* Cold swept my limbs. How often had Edgar stroked my hair, laughingly referred to me as his little black kitten? Revulsion and something indefinable, something strangely sweet, choked me, and Edgar stirred restlessly beside me, one arm flinging over onto my thigh.

I scrambled through the rest of the cards, scanning her words of adoration. Most of the cards she hadn't signed at all.

Valentine's Day. Our lone intersection. This one, like most, wasn't signed. I wondered fruitlessly if she'd written it before or after her visit to Edgar's class.

I find I grow more jealous of our hours, not less, even as a new eternity yawns before us. I am so very tired, but I know in your arms I will reawaken. Bring me home swiftly, sweet. This farewell is familiar but no less bitter.

I stared at the card, confused. She spoke of jealousy, which might have suggested she suspected our lovers' walks, but she didn't mention any fear of another woman who might steal his love away. Had her fatigue been an early symptom of the virus which would steal her away a few weeks later? That didn't seem likely. I didn't think it had so long an incubation period. Perhaps she'd already been weakened by some other illness Edgar hadn't mentioned that left her vulnerable to the ravages of the pandemic. The rest of her words, though, were incomprehensible even at a guess. Some intimate vagary of their relationship, no doubt. How sad, the last written word he had from her was, in fact, a goodbye, though it was written long before she could have known their parting was imminent.

There were only two actual letters in Octavia's assortment.

Neither had been mailed, only had Edgar's name emblazoned across the plain white envelopes. I checked the dates—they'd been written a few months apart, the year they'd married.

I glanced at Edgar, leaning over to look into his dreaming face. My dim bedside lamp cast soft shadows over his prominent jaw and cheekbones, lending him an oddly predatory look even in his sleep. His lashes, though, lay sweetly still and his breathing rumbled regularly. His long fingers still splayed over my lace-clad thigh, clutched occasionally, as though he reached for me even in his dreams.

For me? Or for Octavia? His other kitten. If I was a witchy black cat, Octavia had been a caramel-colored feline, with elegant long fur and those pale green eyes.

Thrusting aside my sudden attack of insecurity and doubt, I unfolded the crackling notebook pages and read them, Octavia's throaty whisper rasping every word in my ear.

CHAPTER ELEVEN

My dearest Edgar,

Even now, it sounds strange to my ears to call you mine. Still, I am hungry to make the claim, and so I challenge all comers. How selfish is that of me? I know of two other hearts whose right to you precedes mine. What sort of monster have I become that I am grateful they were forced by death to relinquish their hold on you so you could be mine? I wish I could say I don't mean it, that I am generous enough to wish Brigitte still lived and I had never seen you as anything other than a patient's husband, but I am not so good a person. I am grateful, at least, that while she lived I hardly saw you, certainly not as a man, only as someone who suffered. I dread to think how wicked my heart might have become if I'd fallen for you while she still breathed.

Does it frighten you, to hear me speak this way? It frightens me. I ought to tell you it is not too late, that I would understand if tomorrow you walk away rather than make your vow to me, but I will not. I can only tell you I love you, madly, deeply, undoingly (I don't think that's a real word.) I can only tell you I will love you always, and I will defend this love to the end of our days, to the depth of my being. If tomorrow you dropped your ring and walked away from me, I would follow you. I would haunt your every hour until you remembered how irresistible you once found me.

Does that sound arrogant? And mad? It must probably be both. But I cannot apologize. My conviction in our love has nothing to do with me. Or at least, not just with me. It's not that I imagine myself so wonderful. It's simply that I have no doubt we are meant for one another. There is no corner of your soul, however dark and dank and cobwebby, that could frighten me. No secret you hold that could dissuade me. I want to fold all your ugliness, your brokenness, your weakness, inside me, until we become a thousand paper swans. And I know, without the slightest hint of fear, that your hands are big enough and strong enough to hold all my shattered pieces, too.

Tomorrow we will make the tired old cliché an undeniable truth. We two will make one. I am so eager for this becoming. I cannot wait to see who I become in your arms. I cannot wait to watch you break apart in mine. Maybe it is only a poor conceit, but I still think these oaths and rings of gold will seal up in us an eternity unbreakable.

My breath caught then, and my eyes filled with tears. How short her eternity had been.

So fear me, my darling. Mock my pretensions, my wild obsession with you, and my certainty I permit

78

you all laughter and doubt. I know it must be so hard to trust in happiness after the terrible losses you have suffered. Perhaps deep down, you only humor me in my adoration and feel little more than gratitude for the occasional distraction I offer from grief. I am untroubled. You are my forever. And I will harbor you, safe in my deep-water port, until you trust your sails to the wind again.

I sign this as your lover, and tomorrow, I will seal these promises as your wife.

Octavia

The pages fluttered to my lap, and I stared blindly into those shadows where I had so often imagined Edgar watched Octavia's ghost wander the foot of our bed.

I'd always regarded marriages with a high degree of skepticism, fed in no little measure by the constant derision it suffers in society. Convenience, sometimes, a vehicle for raising families, an archaic attempt to limit venereal diseases and fatherless children, legal protection, but mostly a hindrance, a liability, a weight that rendered flight impossible. Silly, selfish creature that I was, I thought my marriage to Edgar was something entirely different than what other people attempted. Thought we were nearer to the fairytales and windswept moors and sand-swallowed caverns than anything anyone else might have intended when they slipped on those rings and said those words.

But Octavia's letter proved inarguably how terribly ordinary my heart really was. I flushed to think how different, how precious, I'd imagined our love. Bizarrely, I'd never suffered the least doubt about how Edgar saw me, not even in the weeks before Octavia's illness. And afterward, I'd never questioned my place in his heart was sacred and wholly its own. Now, though, all my affections seemed common and poor beside this wild adoration of Octavia's.

Why, I wondered helplessly, had Edgar even glanced my way? How had I ever caught his eye? What could I possibly offer beside this otherworldly lover who wrote like a poet? I was suddenly, fiercely grateful I'd never had occasion to write Edgar myself. How paltry and plain my words would have been beside these.

Even as my worthlessness swamped me, something stronger, darker, stirred beneath the surface.

Octavia had a way with words, sure, but they stung precisely because I knew how she felt. I understood that unreasoning, indefensible, undeniable hunger. Hadn't I been exactly as terrible a person as she feared she might have been, given the chance? I'd known full well he belonged to another, had never even bothered to excuse myself for my trespass. Still, nothing would have deterred me from pursuing him. Even after I'd met the woman who'd penned these desperate, impassioned words, I'd looked right in her eyes and then spent that very night sharing secrets with her husband on a cold, snowy night.

I was the monster she'd dreaded to become.

Something colder and harder than shame settled in my belly. Neatly, I folded her letter and replaced it, opening her second and final letter. I found the same disparity in her handwriting as I'd seen in the cards. Sometime between the first and second letter, her style became starker, less effervescent. Maybe she'd suffered some unmentioned ailment that cramped her fingers. Perhaps she'd simply found life more urgent, time shorter. I didn't have the same handwriting I'd had in school myself, after all. We all metamorphosize, don't we?

I set aside my rambling thoughts and focused on her words.

My treasured one.

Six months is such a long time to be asleep, but the dawn is worth the night. I would never have chosen our twisted path, but it has its advantages. Life with you will never be dull.

Tomorrow's the anniversary of the day we first met. If we allowed ourselves the indulgence, it would be easy to become creatures of partings, defined by our losses, however brief their power over us. But that is not who we are. For all your love of roots and tables and houses and histories, I know you like me are a true traveler. Together we chase sunrises and open roads and beginnings. I am ready to run!

I paused, reading the same paragraph repeatedly. Try as I might, her meaning escaped me. Did the timeline really make sense? I wasn't sure. I guess I didn't know when Octavia had become one of Brigitte's hospice nurses. But surely that wouldn't be a celebrated anniversary. To my way of thinking, it made more sense to celebrate the night they ran into each other in the wine bar, the first occasion they actually saw each other as man and woman.

Actually, none of the letter made much sense to me. What did she mean about six months of sleep? According to the dates on the letters, this second and last letter had been written just about three months after the wedding. And the rest of her blather simply confused me. Even her tone seemed somehow off—more immediate, less poetic.

Still, I read on. Something in her voice drew me in. Idly I wondered if a person could be hypnotized by simple words on a page. I felt simultaneously dull and light, almost as if I were stoned.

I know you share my hunger. Know you'd swim any depths, wait at any locked courtyard for however long, climb any heights, to reach me. When I'm adrift in the darkness and the awful limbo more black than black, I cling to the certainty that while I cannot see it, your hand is stretched toward mine. When miasmic gusts of despair and disintegration overwhelm me and the void shreds my every thought, I bend all my will toward your bated breath. All I must do is wait, and trust you, and soon what begins as the faintest whisper of a touch on my fingertips will seize my wrist and pull me inexorably back into the light.

Ah. Now I thought I understood. Edgar had never mentioned Octavia struggling with depression, but clearly, that was what she was describing. I certainly couldn't fathom caring for the dying, day in and day out, with no hope of a patient's reprieve.

Still, something flutters inside me, a warning that this respite will be shorter than the last. I fear our mad alchemy costs more than we know. My poor copies fade increasingly in each iteration. But I refuse to own defeat. I will fight for every day I have yet to breathe with you. And if one day our spell seems to have lost its power, I'll find another door to the room where you are. Nothing, certainly not anything so common and crass as death, will ever divide us.

Sympathy swelled, warred with triumph in my belly. I supposed every lover makes the same avowal at some point. We all agree to pretend the inevitable is only for the weak, for the unworthy, for those who fail to love as truly as we do. And then we are all equally surprised when decay strips our bones of all their affectations after all.

Tomorrow we begin our new revolution around the sun. I hope you are ready, my treasure. I intend to wear you out with love. I will retake every inch of your body, claim all your flesh with my kisses, leave my adoration scratched and tattooed deep on your back. I have missed you, oh, I have missed you awful.

Always and forever yours,

Kitten

My lip curled to read that nickname again. I neatly stacked up Octavia's few relics and retied the silver tulle around the little bundle. Beside me, Edgar's heavy, regular breathing attested to untroubled dreams. I suspected my own dreams would be full of feverish darkness and pale jade-green eyes watching me at every turn.

I replaced all the box's contents, put the lid back on. I switched off my reading light and slipped under the cool sheets, my eyes fixed on the dark silhouette of the past on the nightstand beside me. Tomorrow night, I would see what keepsakes Brigitte had left behind. Or perhaps I would spend a little more time with Octavia's voice whispering in my ear. I felt the strangest combination of rivalry and camaraderie with my predecessor.

She, like me, had followed in the footsteps of a ghost wife. She, like me, had thirsted for Edgar with an unreasoning desire that could never be defended to another. She, like me, had been forced to shake off the mantle of the past and seize the happiness of an uncertain future.

Not for the first time, I wondered what had drawn Edgar to me. It wasn't that I questioned his love for me. He surrounded me with words and a myriad of small kindnesses and constant devotion. He didn't just kiss me—he tasted me as if he would draw my soul from my body. But I couldn't deny what a bizarre comparison I made with Octavia. We couldn't possibly have looked more different on the surface. She was grace while I was the elephant in black shit-kickers. She'd been a caretaker of people while I was only a caretaker of books. Despite all this, Edgar and I fit together so neatly, I didn't think another woman could squeeze so much as an exhale between us. We simply belonged to each other, and we didn't need reasons to justify that to ourselves.

My eyes drifted closed. I was wrong to think I would dream of Octavia. I didn't dream at all. It was as if some dark pixie had slid inside the sleeping house of my mind and pulled the blinds shut.

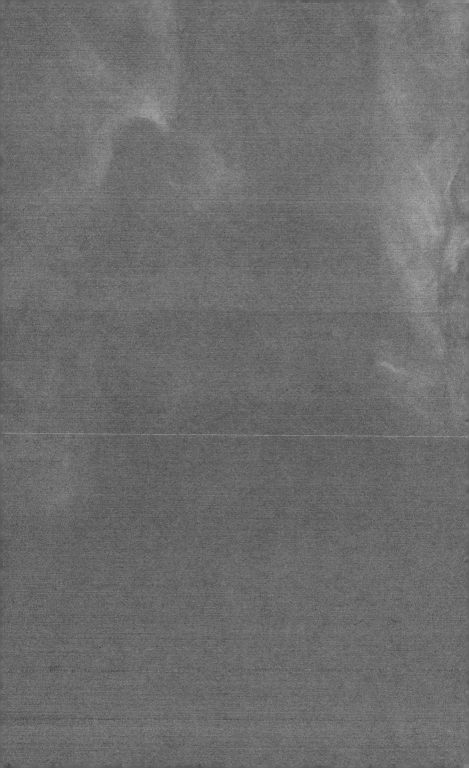

CHAPTER TWELVE

The next morning, I slipped Octavia's photo book into my backpack before filling my thermos of steaming black tea and heading to work. It was getting harder and harder to leave the house. I wasn't sure why, exactly. I wasn't like so many people who quietly loathed their jobs and lived in simmering misery. I didn't spend my days wondering what I should be doing with my life and making half-hearted noises about needing to be more fulfilled.

What more could I want than to spend my days among books? And all the best people wander the stacks. Not those days, of course, but I delighted myself creating personalities and backstories to accompany every list of book requests I filled. I felt like an apothecary to sorcerers, dedicating my days to dispensing all the rare ingredients they required for their spells. Who knew what magic would ensue from the books they read?

All this only made my new malaise that much stranger. I dreaded leaving Edgar behind, and every moment away, my spirit strained toward home. It was ... odd. Wanting to be with a new husband was normal enough, I thought, but I'd never been one of those women who lose all sense of self and interest in friends because some man has a knee-knocker of a kiss. Maybe it wasn't Edgar at all? Maybe I was only infected with some of the wretched dejection the whole world was suffering. This new indolence, whatever its impetus, threatened to treacle all my limbs, and every day I struggled against it less. But today Evan would finally be back at work for the first time since the lockdowns began, and I was eager to see him again.

No hugs for us, of course. Now I wasn't working alone anymore, I was wearing a mask—dark gray cotton with the lower half of a grinning skull emblazoned in black. Evan's, unsurprisingly, was a plain navy blue, an unassuming complement to his white polo shirt and blue jeans. Sweet vanilla Evan. We waved foolishly at each other in the parking lot and walked in together, a safe distance apart.

"So let me see it," he insisted as soon as we'd put our lunches away and switched on the lights.

For a second, I stared at him blankly, wondering how he could have known about the photo book in my bag.

"The ring," he exclaimed impatiently. "Come on. It can't be like you've had many chances to show it off. I still can't believe you up and got married to a stranger I hadn't approved of during quarantine. You do know everyone else is getting divorced, don't you?"

I shrugged. "What can I say? I'm a strict nonconformist."

I waggled my fingers at him with forced cheer.

The ring.

I haven't mentioned it, because it's weirdly uncomfortable. It's not that the rings aren't nice enough. Quite the opposite. The wedding ring was a wide matte polished band of soft, burnished yellow gold. The engagement ring beneath it sported two gleaming sapphires offset around a large, heavy pearl. It looked like something I imagined some French duchess who moonlighted as a dragon-tamer might wear.

It did not look like something you'd pick out for a goth librarian with short, chipped nails and long black box-dyed hair.

And I was pretty sure it hadn't been. Edgar had produced the rings when we'd decided to get married, and even then I hadn't been able to miss how the wedding band matched the slightly wider band he'd never removed after Octavia died. I had no doubt these rings had been Octavia's. They could have even been Brigitte's, once upon a time. I didn't ask, because I didn't want to know.

They were beautiful, after all. What else mattered? It would have been ridiculous to bury them with the dead, equally ridiculous to leave them gathering dust in some jewelry box.

Still, when I brushed a finger over the warm metal as I did a hundred times a day, I couldn't help but feel an echo of my predecessors in the motion, couldn't help imagining it was their fingers I felt curling into my palm. Some mornings I caught myself staring at my lifeline as if it belonged to a stranger, wondering at its intersection, and mildly surprised by the suddenness of its termination. Was I the one inside the skin or outside of it? How many of us were there?

I didn't say any of that to Evan, of course.

He whistled in admiration. "That's gorgeous. I guess you can trade it for quite a bit of ammo and dried goods once the apocalypse commences in earnest, huh?"

I laughed drily. "Obviously my first thought, too."

However reluctant I'd been to leave the house that morning, the day spun away swiftly under the cheer and company Evan brought back to the somber mausoleum the library had become. There wasn't really sixteen hours' worth of work to complete in a day, but neither of us were telling. A scant handful of patrons wandered in, but most people were continuing to limit their exposure and ordering books from home.

While Evan updated the library's social media accounts, I whirled lazily beside him in a spinny chair with Octavia's photo book in my lap. Evan quirked a brow at me as I flipped through the pages.

"You do know how morbid that is, right? And frankly, the mask you're wearing only makes it worse. Are you sure this isn't some Dateline special? I mean, should I be contacting the authorities and suggesting they ought to investigate that poor woman's death?"

"I'm pretty sure you can't fake a pandemic death, especially not one that occurred in the hospital where the husband wasn't even allowed to go."

"Oh, I'm sure he's innocent. You're the likeliest murder suspect. Maybe you dressed up like a nurse and snuck in. Smothered her with a pillow or something. I don't know if even I could recognize you if you changed your hair and makeup. I'm sure no hospital staff could pick you out of a lineup."

I choked on a stifled laugh. "Now I'm worried about you, Evan. Have you been spending all your quarantine planning murders? You do realize your sense of humor is more than a little dark."

Evan grinned at me, unabashed. "You can thank *Forensic Files* and *Homicide Hunter* for my murderous proficiency."

I shrugged. "What I lack in homicidal tendencies I make up for in curiosity. Come on. Be serious. Could you resist the chance to read a lover's ex's letters or look at their pictures? It's like he gave me her Facebook password. You can't expect me to handle that kind of power responsibly."

Evan chuckled. "I guess that's fair. But reading her letters while Edgar lies beside you in bed? That's a road too far, even for me."

"I do know it should feel weirder than it does, but what can I say? We don't have any secrets."

Evan stopped typing at my words and spun in his chair so I could get the full benefit of his skeptical expression. "Everybody has secrets, Sigrun. *Everybody.*"

"Maybe it's a function of the lockdowns," I protested. "We really don't. He's never lied to me about anything. Even when we first met." *When we were cheating*, I didn't say aloud.

"There's more than one way to keep a secret," Evan said. "Sometimes it's not a lie. It's just what you don't say."

I twisted the rings on my left hand. "We talk all the time. About everything." Even as I said it, I knew it wasn't true. We never spoke about the others. But I persisted in my argument all the same as if I only wanted to convince myself it were true.

"You really think you've told him everything important about yourself? There's no dark want or regret you haven't admitted to?"

A strange little terror skittered along my veins as I realized how absolutely I had in fact laid myself bare to Edgar's gaze. "Of course not," I said, forcing casual confidence I didn't feel into my voice. "What's the point of marrying someone who doesn't see you—the real you, the whole you?"

"You really think in just a few weeks, half of which you spent apart and hardly even talking to each other, half of which he was still married to someone else, he got to know all of you?"

A rare anger sparked. I knew it was unreasonable, but that made it no easier to leash. "Coming from the guy who has a strict rule against third dates, how would you even know?"

Evan's eyes widened, but he only spun back to his computer and resumed typing without another word. An apology rushed to my lips, but some darker impulse bit it back. I slammed Octavia's book shut and trounced off to offer unwanted help to an old hippie browsing the hydroponics section.

As fights go, it would hardly register for most people, but Evan and I just didn't argue. We bickered and bothered each other like brother and sister, but even our irritations were mostly fiction. This anger bubbling inside me like a poison felt alien, other, and the discomfort only increased my ire. Knowing it was unwarranted somehow made it stronger. I didn't like this sensation of being pushed out of my own limbs. I blamed Evan. Why did he have to be so pushy, so cynical? Couldn't he just be happy for me? Wasn't that what friends were supposed to do?

An hour later we locked up. The unease continued, and our goodnights were stilted and forced. Something sour twisted in my belly as I drove away. Why hadn't I just apologized? Or teased Evan back into his good graces? I'd known when I said it that it was a cheap shot. Evan was ace, and while he wanted a relationship, he'd been on the receiving end of too much disappointment and dismay to easily risk it again. He was like a cat that wanted to swim but couldn't quite convince itself to do more than shake a paw out over the water. He'd nearly married his best friend from high school, and since that disastrous breakup, he'd been more or less on his own. I knew he was lonely, and I knew he was trying, and still I'd twisted the knife. I was disgusted with myself.

It didn't help that a colder voice whispering from the back of my mind insisted the problem was his, and not mine. He shouldn't have thought he could question what Edgar and I shared. After all, what I'd said might have been mean, but it was still true. Evan didn't know what a real committed relationship was like. He certainly didn't know what it was like to hunger and thirst after a touch, a glance, a taste. What it was like to ache for the moment flesh melted into flesh and became flame.

I shook my head. Even now, heat pooled between my thighs and my breath caught. More and more, it seemed the hours between our joinings passed in a haze. Only our time together felt real. Everything else was a mist I endured until I could breathe clear air again.

So Evan was feeling a little pissy. He'd get over it. After all, we were just work friends. He needed to understand there were boundaries to our relationship.

I frowned. That didn't sound right. Didn't feel right. I'd never exactly been a fan of rules or fences or walls.

Some prizes need protecting.

"Fine!" I snapped out loud, startling myself into stomping on the brake at a yellow light I definitely should have accelerated through. Behind me, squealing tires and an infuriated honk agreed. Weakly, I waved a remorseful hand out the window.

"I'll just alienate my best friend right when I need him the most, shall I?" I muttered sarcastically.

A real friend wouldn't be jealous of your happiness.

"Ha! Jealous. As if. He doesn't understand, that's all. He's worried about me. That's what friends do. They worry."

Worry? Or undermine. Or sabotage.

"That's a little melodramatic, don't you think?"

A second, longer honk yanked me out of my reverie to see the light was green again. *Damn it.* What was wrong with me? I've always been prone to talking to myself, but solitary shouting matches had never been on the roster before. I needed to get a grip.

I'd apologize to Evan tomorrow, I promised myself.

CHAPTER THIRTEEN

But I didn't.

I intended to. I had all the words ready on the tip of my tongue, but when I walked up to the front door, keys a-jangle, and saw the hesitancy in his eyes, a cruel instinct I didn't even know I possessed swallowed the apology whole.

"Good morning, Evan," I offered in a cool voice I scarcely recognized as my own instead.

The hesitancy vanished, and a terse defensiveness took its place. Evan had never looked at me that way before.

"Good morning," he responded in kind.

It was a long day. I decided to replace all the peeling Dewey Decimal and alphabetical labels on the shelves, a task which should have taken me at least a week and given me a good reason to avoid my coworker.

My friend? I rolled the words around and found they tasted bitter.

Evan handled all the peopling, a task for which he was eminently better suited than me at any time. He had a gift for putting people at ease—or was it just the gift of gab, I thought snidely.

By the time I made it home that night, I was thoroughly out of sorts. If you can imagine a menstrual wet cat with stickers caught in its fur, that was me walking in the front door. Edgar came whistling out of the kitchen, lifting a glass of wine to his lips. He took one look at me and reversed course without a word.

By the time I'd gotten my shoes off and hung up my coat—an unnecessarily complicated affair which involved me snapping one hanger in half and swearing at the next—he'd reappeared with a second glass of wine and suitably abashed expression on his face.

As it turns out, it's hard to yell at someone for no reason while gulping wine. Much to Edgar's benefit.

"Up to the bath with you," he ordered me sternly. "And then it's dinner in bed for you."

I did not argue.

Wine and steaming bubbles and the impossibly sweet, heady scent of jasmine vanilla scoured away all the grit and grime and regretful grief of the day. Funny how a fragrance I once would have found nauseatingly cloying had become my cue to unwind and let go. I was feeling entirely myself, absolutely lovely in my skin by the time I lifted my heat-pink body from the water and wrapped myself up in the thick cashmere-soft robe Edgar had given me. A pale sky-blue—not exactly my style, but I couldn't deny how the shade complemented my dark hair and fair complexion. More importantly, it was delightfully warm and cozy.

Our bedroom was illuminated only by my bedside lamp and a handful of fat candles. Edgar had a tray table by my side of the bed with a glass of water and the rest of the bottle of wine.

"No food?" I pouted.

With one hand he tugged at the belt of my robe so it fell away to reveal my naked body beneath. His other hand cupped the back of my head, tugging almost painfully at my wet hair as he tilted my face up to meet his.

"It's so hard to wait for you," he growled before his mouth covered mine.

The moment he touched me, everything else disappeared. I clung to him as he kissed me as if the ground itself had dropped away and only his strength kept me from vanishing. My lips were bruised—I think they may have been bleeding. One of his broad hands twisted painfully in my hair, the other held my hips pressed against him. He lifted his mouth only to plunder my throat, with bites and kisses and tender laps of his tongue. Terror tantalized and excited me, and when he flung me down onto the bed, I opened for him without hesitation.

There was nothing sweet about this lovemaking. It was all desperation and longing and a kind of mad violence that only heightened every sensation of pleasure. I thought I would break—I was frightened he had. But when it was over, elation swept over me and I rose over his sweating, gleaming chest like some conquering marauder claiming my spoils. I saw the same exultation I could feel pounding in my veins shining in his eyes as he laughed breathlessly up at me.

"Quit your job," he said. "You never have to leave this bed again."

All my air whooshed out of me, and I leaned my palms against his breastbone.

"What?" I couldn't process the words.

"Quit your job."

"But—" I scrambled to make sense of his words. "You're not even working right now. And my job—I love my job."

But the words sounded much weaker than I expected them to. I did love my job, didn't I?

I did. Of course I did.

"I have plenty of money to carry us through this little interruption. The restaurant will open up again soon. And it's not as if people will stop reading books just because you aren't at the library anymore. Brad or Bart or whatever your friend's name is will carry on for you."

"Evan," I supplied automatically, even while my mind searched fruitlessly for some resistance, some counterargument to his suggestion.

"Evan will find books and answer questions and watch his life drift away from him. No need for you to do that."

I punched his shoulder, but the gesture was empty, and he

knew it. I ought to have been offended, I ought to have been furious. I knew I ought to have been.

But all I felt was the heat radiating from his trapped thighs against mine, his coarse hair rasping against my skin, the promise of renewed pleasure swelling within me. What was it I was supposed to be angry about again?

We made love a second time, a little slower but no less starved. His words sank into my skin, and somehow the possibility of not working took on a patina I'd never glimpsed before. He was right, I told myself. I wasn't some first-responder without whom the pandemic world would suffer. If I didn't go to work at the library, Meghan or Derek would take my place. Sigrun wasn't the last stitch holding the universe together—if she walked out of the madness the world had become and never looked back, who would even notice?

Okay, now *that* was a warning sign. I did not intend to become one of those weirdos who referred to themselves in the third person.

But the point was valid. And right now, catching my breath in the cool sheets while Edgar traced the outline of my breasts with a feather touch, more time to spend in bed sounded like an eminently good idea.

"All right," he rumbled. "You clean up. Again. I'll go bring up that food you were begging for."

"Oh, yes." I laughed. "Food. I remember food."

It was only seven in the evening, but I hardly stirred from bed the rest of the night. Edgar brought up some sort of chicken dish baked in a crust, made with ginger and mint and a white wine sauce. Caramelized onions and garlic added a delightful touch. Naked under the sheets, I pulled the covers up to hide my substantial food belly. Edgar puttered around, cleaning the kitchen, wiping down my tray table, and exchanging my bottle of wine for an icy after-dinner vodka. He preferred port or Scotch but humored my less-refined tastes.

"There are benefits," he sometimes teased me, "to a cheap date."

Social media, which had become a haven and home for so

many over the lockdowns, now bored me terribly. It was all the same. Politics, religion, puppies, and posts about exactly how they'd gained their quarantine fifteen. If I was extra unlucky, somebody had just gotten a box of makeup in the mail they had to unbox and apply in front of a camera. Gods and goddesses save me. People who had so little faith in anything else still possessed endless faith in their own fascination.

At first, I took refuge in the cold comfort of crazy conspiracy theories and stayed well on the Sasquatch-and-aliens side of the internet, but it didn't take long for racists and bigots to suck all the fun out of simple looney-tune land, too. So I hardly ever updated my status anymore.

Happily, I had a near-inexhaustible store of romance novels. I had a friend at the local bookstore who kept me in stripped paperbacks, and I regularly combed the library sales for worn novels whose scuffed pages bore witness to their engrossing content. One night spent relaxing and reading in bed was hardly evidence of my complete debauchery, I told myself.

The little plate of milk-chocolate dipped blackberries Edgar slid onto my tray table did nothing to exonerate me, but I finished off every one all the same.

That night, though, my lycanthropic murder mystery failed to hold my attention. Again and again, my gaze slipped from the page to the paper-wrapped box on my nightstand.

I'd met Octavia in her own words. Felt her heart beating in my hands as she spilled her feelings artlessly on the page. What sort of woman had Brigitte been? Would I find more of myself in her artifacts than I had in Octavia's?

CHAPTER FOURTEEN

I t was funny. I'd just tucked my novel under the bed and lifted the lid from the box Edgar had gifted me when he strolled in the door. I had the oddest—and silliest—sensation he'd been standing there, waiting for me.

"Oh," I stumbled over my words, unsure whether I should feel self-conscious or not. The vodka said no. Any other voice I might claim seemed fainter and fainter these days. "I didn't see you there."

In the shadowy, flickering candlelight, his eyes glittered. His mouth twisted, but his words were soft.

"Go ahead," he urged me, coming around to his side of the bed. He stripped as I watched him. "I'm going to take a shower before I come to bed. Are you reading Brigitte?"

I nodded mutely.

I can't explain it even now, but there was the dearest intimacy in the question. He was sharing the grave wrappings of a beloved. I'd tried to pretend nothing more than lurid curiosity drove me when I'd told Evan about the gift he'd given me, but I couldn't lie to myself. This was sacred. This was trust. Whatever misgivings Evan had, whatever secrets he was so sure persisted, couldn't compare with the raw vulnerability of this offering.

Edgar leaned across the pillows and kissed my forehead. The bathroom door snicked quietly closed behind him.

Brigitte's little bundle was wrapped in a black Ramones T-shirt. *Ah*, I thought. Here she is. This'll be my girl.

I don't know why it was so important to me to find some point of commonality with Edgar's previous lovers. I think I was looking for some validation, some reassurance he hadn't made a terrible mistake with me, that I was more than a heedless rebound he was sure to regret.

How little I understood then.

Brigitte's handwriting was nothing like Octavia's curling script. Her hand was bold, incisive, impatient. I could easily imagine the woman behind these thick black strokes deciding without hesitation she'd rather lose both her breasts than her life. How tragic that such a courageous act had won her nothing in the end.

I placed Brigitte's photobook alongside the pile of pages, examined her face for something familiar. Physically, she was nothing like me, and nothing like Octavia either. Lean and nearly as tall as me, with shoulder-length chestnut hair she normally wore in two short ponytails behind her ears. Even now, she looked as if she might walk right out of the pages, all coiled energy and fierce strength. Almost all her photos were taken outdoors. She'd been a biker, a runner, a climber. I thought of what little I knew of the restaurant business. She seemed to possess the perfect personality that would thrive in such a high-stress, fast-paced environment, and the night owl schedule allowed her more daylight hours for playtime.

I wondered if Edgar missed what looked to have been a constant buzz of hardcore physical activities. Walking from a bookstore to a coffee shop was about as athletic as I ever wanted to be. He gave no hint of restlessness or dissatisfaction. I told myself he'd been much younger when he and Brigitte were together. Maybe as he'd gotten older, he'd found himself content with moonlit walks and bedroom calisthenics.

Brigitte's mementos consisted mostly of stickers from various state parks, craft brewery coasters, and champagne corks. I sniffed the dark edges of the corks as if I could evoke the memories they held. What occasions had they celebrated, what giddy celebrations had called for bubbles?

I closed my eyes and gave myself over to images of a younger Edgar laughing over champagne flutes into a pair of flashing brown eyes. For an instant, I could have sworn those eyes looked past him and landed right on me. A cold hand seized my heart and squeezed it so tight I could hardly breathe. My eyelids flew open on a gasp, and I saw Edgar watching me from the bathroom doorway, a bemused expression on his face.

"All right there?"

I dropped the champagne cork in my hand. "Just woolgathering," I muttered, feeling my cheeks heat.

He nodded toward the corks as he slid into bed beside me. Tonight, he was reading some comparison of Churchill and Orwell. I could never quite identify his reading interests.

"Brigitte never had the luxury of imagining herself immortal, so she liked to celebrate every chance she got. Half-birthdays, the first bike ride of the year, the day the jack-o-lantern finally rotted and had to be thrown out, every tattoo she got, first snows."

I was intrigued. "Tattoos?" Another intersection we shared.

Edgar chuckled. "She had quite a few. They're all in there." He gestured toward her photobook.

"Ah."

He plumped up his pillow and disappeared behind the cover of his book. Brigitte had not been the sentimental sort, it appeared. Where Octavia had resorted to Hallmark on every occasion, Brigitte's few missives were hastily scrawled on torn sheets of paper or sticky notes. Some she had dashed off so quickly, her handwriting might have belonged to another woman altogether. I read them all, hungry for clues to her personality, but she gave little away. She had been all life out loud, I thought, leaving nothing to be hoarded on paper. Perhaps living with such a present threat of death had left her loath to create her own relics. You can't decide what to leave behind without first resigning yourself to leaving.

I was sitting cross-legged in a pile of blankets, my back to the end of the bed. I watched Edgar's book wavering and knew he was falling asleep. Without knowing why, I waited until he surrendered, switching off his bedside lamp and turning his back to me, his breathing almost instantly reverting to the sonorous rhythm of sleep after he murmured a drowsy, "Goodnight, Kitten."

Now it was just me and the ghosts I was gathering, gazing on each other through the shadows with patient eyes.

If anyone had told me a year ago, I would be married to a man with not one or two but three dead lovers, that I would be wearing the rings and sleeping beneath the sheets of the departed, that all my thoughts and hours would be consumed with their thoughts, their histories, their memories, I'd have sworn they were mad. But the reality of it was nothing like you would imagine. I was not jealous, or resentful, or afraid.

I was hungry. I wanted to know them, not as characters in stories Edgar might tell or as wraiths remembered by his friends and family, but as the whole, living women they had been. I wanted to somehow subsume them, take them into myself, and give them air. I wanted Edgar's love for me to be the culmination of every love he'd experienced. I didn't want to just make him happy. I wanted to make him whole. I wanted to embody his every dream and desire and memory.

The arrogance of that hardly occurred to me. I told myself my burgeoning self-confidence was the result of Edgar's constancy. You might wonder how I could find security in the arms of a man that had just as tenderly held so many others, but my faith could not be swayed. Edgar and I belonged together, and that assurance anchored me in the world as nothing else had.

I flipped through Brigitte's photo book until I found the section devoted to her tattoos. Edgar had not exaggerated. Colorful ink covered both her slender arms and graced the flat canvas of her chest. Unlike mine, which tended more toward symbols, Brigitte's tattoos were mostly a combination of flamboyant tropical flowers and wild animals, drawn with an exquisite level of photo-realism. She was a garden, I thought, not some well-tamed Japanese cultivation but a savage Garden of Eden.

Vining trumpet lilies in riotous green and orange curled around her ankles and up her calves as if they seized her. One tattoo, smaller than the rest and solitary in its canvas high on her left thigh, sent an icy shudder rippling over my skin.

A kitten, caught in a playful cavort, its likeness similar to the Victorian ephemera seen in old greeting cards and advertisements.

I lowered the book to my lap, traced the feline outline with a shaking hand. It didn't mean anything, I told myself. So she had a kitten tattoo. They couldn't be that unusual. So what if it was the only domesticated animal she'd chosen? So what if it was drawn in an entirely different style than the rest of her tattoos? Maybe it was the first one she'd gotten, when she was younger and not sure of her own style yet.

Lots of people made completely random choices with their tattoos. Sometimes they didn't even have any particular story or meaning behind them, people just liked them, thought they were pretty or funny or shocking enough to merit some real estate. So, what if the rest of Brigitte's work felt like a cohesive work of art?

There was certainly nothing to indicate she'd gotten this tattoo after she'd met Edgar.

But I knew she had, all the same.

Why did it bother me so much? I couldn't say. Logically, I knew people tended to use the same endearments indiscriminately, be they *dear, honey, darlin',* or *babe.* But *kitten* felt different to me. It felt personal, distinctive, deliberate. It was almost as though Edgar were summoning a former love when he called me by what increasingly felt like her name and not mine. As if I were only a voodoo doll he used to reach a lost soul.

I slammed the book shut and shook my head. Edgar stirred and muttered in his sleep but didn't wake. I was being ridiculous, I scolded myself half-heartedly. Edgar had never treated me like his fourth choice, his consolation prize. He'd given me no reason to suspect him of anything but the sincerest affections.

No reason other than calling me by another lover's pet name, my brain pointed out coldly.

I wrapped Brigitte's things back in her old T-shirt. I was pleased to see my hands had stopped shaking, though I kept my eyes averted from the last and largest bundle left in the box. Maybe Evan was right. Maybe there was something too gory and morbid about this strange anthropology, even for me. I'd told myself this was about understanding Edgar better, seeing past the shadows into his secret heart so I could keep it safe, but what if I was wrong? Maybe the heart really does keep sacred some spaces only a fool dares trespass. Maybe I should let Octavia and Brigitte and Devlin rest in peace.

I turned off my reading light and laid down, pulling the covers over my shoulders and wrapping my arms around my knees. My heartbeat thudded in my ear resting on the pillow, like footsteps chasing me down a dark corridor, footsteps that thudded faster as my breaths shortened. I must be trapped in an Edgar Allan Poe poem, I thought wildly, suddenly convinced it wasn't my own heart I heard.

It was Devlin's heart, pounding away in the box on my bedside table. Devlin, with her fat stack of letters I feared and longed to read. Devlin, Edgar's first love, maybe his last love.

His only love, the words welled up wickedly in my throat.

With a gasp, I turned, wrapping myself around Edgar's warm, substantial body that brought me wonderfully back into my own. He stirred but didn't wake, one of his large hands drawing mine to his bare chest and holding me fast. I fell asleep tangled up in him, the steady rhythm of his heart under my hand the undercurrent of dreams I couldn't remember when I woke.

CHAPTER FIFTEEN

I put in my two weeks' notice at the library the next day. It only made sense. We don't live to work, after all: we work to live, and if Edgar wasn't worried about money there was no need for me to be. With Edgar, in our beautiful home with the richly carved moldings, the wide paned windows, the bookshelves and the paintings and the sculptures, was where my joy lived. Who when offered a castle would rather spend her days in a scullery? Not to mention that whatever precautions we took, I was still at more risk for the virus than if I stayed home. Edgar had already lost one wife to this horrid illness. He could not bear to lose another.

It only made sense.

Evan disagreed, of course. He didn't say so, but I could see it in his eyes. I was tempted to provoke him, to dare him to argue with me, but I managed to wrestle down the contrary impulse. He did ask me why, and when I flippantly said, "It makes me happy," I saw something move in his eyes, something I thought I ought to recognize but couldn't quite place.

He only said, "I thought you loved the library."

I rolled my shoulders, suddenly fidgety. "I love books," I responded, hearing the waspish tone but unable to restrain it. "I don't need this building for that."

He nodded and kept sorting the returns onto a cart. My words felt like a lie, but they couldn't be, could they? Protestations niggled in my brain, faintly insisting there was far more to the profession

I'd chosen than a simple love of books. Being a librarian was about the free dissemination of knowledge in all its mediums, about helping people access resources, about connecting students and archives, about service to people and to the broadening of a common understanding. It was far from some solitary and selfish enclosure of the self in pages.

But those protests felt farcical, like false fronts propped up by a stranger. Some other woman, who needed high-minded causes and constant external validation to justify her existence, for whom simple want wasn't a fair enough justification for taking. Elation, more powerful than these paltry doubts, bubbled within me. I had the strongest sensation my life was only just beginning, and it was a beautiful, beautiful life. Evan's sulk, as I considered it, couldn't dim my joy. I felt liberated. Loosed of chains I'd only just realized I was wearing.

The cocktail of urgency and dread that had sloshed sickeningly in my stomach the night before at the thought of reading Devlin's letters subsided. I would wait, I decided, until I'd completed my last day at the library. I didn't have a reason, exactly. It just seemed fitting, somehow, to bid goodbye to one chapter before reading another.

Edgar was delighted I'd given notice. I could sense the same effervescence I felt fizzing in his veins, too. Those were halcyon days: we were dandelion wishes adrift on a summer breeze, certain their journey ended in joy. I no longer found him staring stone-eyed into invisible shadows or hunched dry-sobbing into his hands. Our home smelled always of yeast and warm sugar and jasmine vanilla.

My last day at the library, I was stunned to find Evan had organized a virtual going-away party for me. He'd strung the break-room with black streamers and black and silver balloons. The cake looked like a Halloween feast, festooned with black cobwebs and spiders with sparkling red eyes. A banner read, *We'll Miss You!* He'd even managed to sort the entire library staff into a Zoom meeting. Green punch I could have sworn featured a dash of absinthe filled little plastic champagne flutes.

I couldn't keep the tears from swimming in my eyes when I met Evan's gaze across the room. We'd hardly even spoken a word the last two weeks outside of necessary professional conversations. Fear I hadn't realized was waiting in my belly rushed into my throat, and for a moment I panicked, staring around at the emblems of my exit like a prisoner bound for the gallows stares at his cell as he is dragged away.

"Evan?" I croaked.

He crossed the room, pulling me into a tight hug. I was struck for an instant by his clean soap-and-linen smell. The strongest sensation, of being suspended between two powerful forces, sent shivers chasing down my spine.

"It's not too late," he whispered against my hair, his warm breath in my ear like the sea reminding the shell of its birthplace. "You can stay if you want."

Something struck, again and again, in my chest, flint against steel. Sputter, sputter—and spark.

I shoved him back as cold seas rushed into my eyes. "I am doing what I want," I told him. "Why would I stay here?"

I flung a hand at the chipped paint on the cinderblock wall, the decorations that had looked so festive earlier now appearing tawdry and pathetic. Evan shook his head and walked away from me, sticking a fork right in the cake and taking a big bite. He muttered something I couldn't hear into the frosting, and I spun around and went back to shelving novels.

I crammed all my knickknacks into a cardboard box that afternoon—frayed bookmarks from authors I'd met, my yarn voodoo doll collection and the creepy scarecrow Evan had given me last Halloween. I hesitated over a photo of him and me dressed as giant novels from last year's annual Harvest Parade. It was corny and hilarious and ridiculous. Unlike Edgar, who filled every room he entered, Evan had no presence at all. It had been one of the things I loved most about him. Where other men postured and pounded their chests,

Evan just was and was perfectly comfortable in his own skin.

As I stared at his crudely yellow-painted grinning face, his arms spread wide across the covers of *Roll of Thunder, Hear My Cry,* contempt closed my throat and curled my lips. I shoved the photo into the box. Evan might be happy in this little world with its little walls, but not me.

I tossed him my library keys and strode out the door ahead of him at closing time. He'd hardly acknowledged I breathed since the debacle in the breakroom. But when I closed the trunk of my car and turned, he stood behind me, his hands stuffed awkwardly in his khaki pockets. I knew disdain burned in my gaze, and I didn't bother to shutter it.

He saw, but didn't answer it. Instead, nothing but a steady compassion burned in his eyes as he spoke softly. "I'm worried about you, Sigrun. Call me if you need me. You're never going to be too far away."

I managed a hoarse laugh, though even I didn't know what was funny. "Don't sit by the phone. I'll see you around."

I cried all the way home. I didn't know why I did that, either.

In the driveway, I dug through my glove compartment for spare napkins. I nearly started crying again when I recognized them from the last time, months ago, when Evan and I had gone to the ice cream shop for double-dip waffle cones after work. I sopped up my dripping mascara and grabbed a pencil to retrace the heavy black lines around my eyes before heading inside.

I didn't know why it was important Edgar not suspect me of a single regret, but it was. I redrew the mahogany lipstick I'd gnawed off on my way home. As the creamy paste dragged across my bottom lip, that same spark roared back to life, and all inclination to tears vanished.

My thick-heeled boots announced my return with panache as I stomped into the entryway. "Honey, I'm home," I yelled as gaily as if my momentary tears belonged to a stranger. "Home for always."

Edgar appeared with an icy-cold pink martini topped with a rose petal. "The conquering hero returns," he said, presenting the glass with a flourish.

A sip suggested jasmine gin and a hint of strawberry. My favorite.

Wait a minute. Was that right? Didn't I prefer vodka martinis? Hesitantly, I took another sip.

Oh, no. This was delicious. What had I been thinking? So much upheaval in a single day had me discombobulated. Delicate, fruity, and bitter—nothing surpassed these flavors.

Edgar watched me, his dark eyes burning intensely into mine as if his tongue tasted the liquor just as mine did. The moment the glass left my lips, he seized me and kissed me as if I'd been gone a century instead of only a few hours. His teeth tugged at my bottom lip, and pleasure speared hotly through me. I wrapped my hands around the back of his neck and drew him close when he would retreat, drinking at his mouth as if my soul depended on it.

When we finally parted, panting and wide-eyed, he gestured to the box I'd dropped haphazardly on the foyer floor.

"Probably mostly trash," I said by way of explanation. "I had to get my stuff out of there." It was funny. My few possessions, so carefully hoarded and displayed over the last few years, suddenly seemed the debris of a woman I barely remembered. I pushed them to the wall with my foot, slipped out of my boots with a rushing relief.

"I think I'll take a bath," I said.

"Dinner will be ready when you are," Edgar told me.

As the hot water ran and the bubbles foamed, I scrubbed the makeup off my face with an impatient hand. I felt like a clown escaping the circus. I needed to get this costume off me, step into the cool night as only myself.

I shut off the taps before the water could spill over and slipped down the hall, indulging a powerful impulse I could neither explain nor deny.

I stood in front of the guest bedroom closet. My eyes skipped over the tiny pastel affairs the diminutive Octavia had sported during daylight hours and clung to the extravagant Victorian-style gowns of transparent white silk and lace, with their mutton-chop sleeves and thigh-high lace inserts trailing the ground.

I didn't even know where a person would buy such a fantastic indulgence. And I don't think I'd worn white since I was six months old. But still, I pulled the frothy confection from its hanger and took it back to the bathroom with me.

Sounds macabre, doesn't it? Not just to wear a dead woman's clothes, but to wear a dead woman's lingerie? It didn't feel like that, though. It felt like reclaiming what had been mine all along, only mine.

I took a long bath. I traced the path of the glistening bubbles down my pale skin as if I'd never looked at my own limbs before. I dug my fingers deep into my masses of hair as I lathered the fragrant shampoo. I wiped away the steam of the bathroom mirror when I emerged from the scalding water and took scissors to my locks, chopping them off just below my ears. I rubbed the flowery lotion into my tender pink skin, feeling every cell awaken beneath my fingers.

Silk and lace whispered over my shoulders, across my wide hips, my generous thighs. I flattened my palms over my belly, settling deep into my bones.

"Hello there," I murmured to the stranger in the mirror. Unfamiliar, but still the same. I smiled to see her emerge, as whole and powerful as ever she was.

When I walked into the kitchen, Edgar's greeting echoed mine. "There you are," he said, his eyes glittering almost as if with tears. "Hungry?"

"Starving."

He crossed the room in two strides, bent me over his broad arm, and filled me up.

CHAPTER SIXTEEN

don't think there's any more delightful sensation than the wonderful soreness of being well-used, well-abused, well-awoken, well-imbibed. I sat cross-legged in our tangled sheets as Edgar slept the sleep of the utterly sated and counted the beautiful bruises and bite-marks on the inside of my thighs. Silk and lace floated around my soft belly where I'd pulled up my skirts. I loved seeing his touch branded on my skin. My thoughts were a little muddy, a little confused, but pleasure suffused them all. I'd held nothing back, and he'd taken it all as if his life depended on it.

"Devlin," I tried the name out softly. Tongue and lips wrapped around the syllables. The strangest thing, but I could almost taste her lips under mine. I wondered, in the most scattered way, if those were Edgar's teeth that had sunk so deep in my flesh or if they were hers.

I lifted the lid to the box by my bed and withdrew her thick bundle of letters.

My treasure, she wrote. I caught my breath. If it was odd Edgar called us all kitten, surely it was odder that Devlin and Brigitte and Octavia all called him Treasure.

Patience! I haven't any. Patience is for the dead and the sleeping. I am neither and don't intend to ever be. Why do people die, anyway? They 'give up the ghost?' Well, I refuse. Death might well knock at my door, but I'll send him away with a broom at his backside.

This is good news for you. You said last night you could never have enough days with me. Leave all maudlin talk for these mortal bone-bags who stumble from one chemical reaction to the next. You and I—we're more than that. Because we choose to be.

Am I scaring you? I hope so. A little fear is good for the soul. When did people decide safety was the thing? Everything we crave is in the scary places. Want a fish? Brave the waters. Want a buffalo? You gotta run with the beasties. Want love? Leave that insipid potion to the poets. I'm about belonging. Owning. Keeping.

You know the first gasp of terror when you drop off a cliff before you catch yourself and haul yourself back up to solid ground? I want to live in that gasp. I want you to drink that stolen fallen air out of my mouth and laugh when you realize we're flying.

A walk on the roof of the university chem lab might not have been much of a first date, but it's a damn good beginning for a story that doesn't end.

I'll meet you back on the roof tonight. You bring the gin, and I'll bring the flowers.

Kitten

I closed my eyes and raised the page to my face as if I could breathe in that long-ago night. I could see them, Edgar and Devlin, dark silhouettes scarcely outlined by faintest starshine and campus streetlights, tripping and laughing along the edge of a towering gray stone hall. I could see *us*. I could smell the gin, taste its sharpness on my tongue as cool night air shushed across my laughing mouth. I looked with amazement at my strong, long-boned fingers as they shredded rose petals and scattered them over the edge of the roof. I shoved playfully at Edgar's broad chest, chortling shamelessly at the terror surging into his eyes as he lost his footing. I grabbed his hand, yanked him back toward me, and his mouth fell over mine, exacting wonderful, terrible penance for my wickedness.

Oh, Edgar. How sweet and dear and pure you were then, before loss plunged its dark talons into your heart and filled your vision with shadows of all my absences.

My gaze cleared, and I became aware of the dryness in my mouth, a dull pounding in my head. The gray dawn crept across the floor. Had I fallen asleep? I frowned, dismayed by the wanton frivolity of my imagination. It was becoming increasingly difficult to find the lines between the real world and the dreaming. Was it possible, after all, to read too much? I had been retreating deeper into my novels and books of fairytales and legends, from Yggdrasil to the Mabinogion to the Arthurian cycles. Stories had always seemed more real and substantive to me than the grown-up silliness of piling from one box into a box with wheels to reach yet another box, to trade bits of paper and plastic for pretend food and call it all fulfillment. It was a thousand times easier to believe in the fae than in the Federal Reserve.

Or maybe I was only removing the veil that had blinded me. I'd thought Edgar lost when I found him gazing black-eyed into corners, but what if he'd been staying where life really breathed? What if I was only just now waking up to what mattered?

I lifted the stack of letters from my lap and looked at the fingerprints already purpling on my skin. *There.* This was real.

What stranger magic was there, after all, than language itself? Tiny, indefinite marks that trap sound, sound that traps meaning, meaning that traps existence, and all of it held like hoarded gold on the stretched skin of tree-wraiths. If that were true, it could hardly be impossible to believe Devlin's sensations found an answering echo in my flesh.

That dizzying, boneless fever gripped me more often these days, swept over my skin, and I was consumed by the longing to sleep again, to dream, to lose myself in some plane thoroughly divorced from skin and bones. I pushed the box haphazardly off onto the floor, never minding when Brigitte's and Octavia's bundles half-slid onto the carpet. I clutched Devlin's pages to my chest and tumbled into sleep the moment my eyes closed.

But when I woke, I remembered no dreams at all. A querulous little voice insisted that should trouble me, but it didn't.

Edgar brought me a late breakfast of hot croissants and butter and fresh raspberries. My nose failed to warn me of a switch before I absently sipped from the steaming cup, and I sputtered when my tongue encountered creamy coffee instead of my usual English Breakfast tea. I started to protest—I'd never been a coffee drinker, and I wasn't entirely convinced the clock hands could move without some impetus from tea leaves. But I found myself gingerly taking another sip first. *Hmm.* It really wasn't so bad. Perhaps I'd never really given it a chance. I'd never had an actual French chef make it for me before.

I curled up in Edgar's wingback leather chair, wrapped his lambswool blanket around my bare feet, and returned to poring over Devlin's letters. He left me to it, doing I don't know what downstairs. Strains of Vivaldi drifted through the house, evoking at once tranquility and a strange titillation. I gave myself up to Devlin's words and believed everything her voice murmured in my ears.

Treasure,

I have the strangest feeling, like we're in a waiting room or a lobby somewhere. I love chemistry, but school's not the thing— it's just a placeholder for whatever comes next. I can't imagine what that is, but I also can't wait. All I know is, whatever waits, waits for us both.

It's usually such fun to play the dating games, but I'm horribly bored with them now. I should play hard to get, I suppose, but you and I both know I'm only hard to get rid of. Most people look their whole lives for someone like you, for someone like me, for a fit like ours, and even if they do stumble across it, they lose it or give it up or never see it at all.

People—oh, people bore me too. They're all the same. Gray-faced little automatons, waking up when the alarm says so, working as long as the boss says so, buying whatever the commercials tell them to buy, mowing their damn lawns, and waxing their eyebrows. They don't LIVE. They barely even breathe.

But we're not like that. We're going to taste it all. Use ourselves up like old rags and then start over again. I'm going to be wildly jealous, you know. I have a temper like a wet cat and I despise mornings, but I will love you so hard you'll thank me when your bones break. We're going to make all those old romances look about as exciting as pharmaceutical warnings.

I dreamed about you last night. I dream about you every night now, I think. It's quite lovely— like walking out of one room into another and finding everything you loved best in both. I may have to tell you goodnight here, but I know when I open my eyes in the dark, you'll be there waiting for me on the other side.

Still, I'd rather wake up beside you. Soon enough. No! Never soon enough. I hate these stupid dorm rooms. Just a few more weeks, and we'll be in our own place.

Unless I wind up in prison for killing my roommate. Insipid little snot.

You have to call me as soon as you find this letter! I'm running out of places to hide these. You always find them so fast. I must get more devious.

Kitten

CHAPTER SEVENTEEN

As luck would have it, *La Table* reopened a couple of days after my last day at the library. Some restaurants had opened earlier at a 25% capacity, but the owner hadn't thought *La Table*'s overhead could sustain such a low customer count. He'd waited till the state okayed the 50% capacity. They'd pulled out fifteen tables and spaced pairs of bar stools six feet apart.

The streets maintained a surreal stillness as if the little hunches of masked pedestrians darting door to door were only ghosts after all. Based on what I could gather from the news, the virus wasn't any less dangerous or deadly than it had ever been, but people were losing patience with being cooped up. Suddenly all the movie representations of the Black Plague seemed wildly unrealistic. Had people really avoided the houses of the infected and fled the cities in terror? I had the feeling most people today would rather sound off in a line and just jettison every thirtieth person or so into their grave if it meant the rest of them could still attend a concert or catch a movie.

The farmers' market where Edgar got most of his vegetables and some specialty items like local honey and mead were barely functional, but Edgar simply went to the individual farms and collected his ingredients that way. I went with him, staying in the car to reduce exposure while he carried crates of goods out and filled the trunk and the backseat. The warm smells of dirt and living things tickled my nose and made me smile.

I hadn't realized how small my world had become until we

were flying down country roads and watching the verdant Oregon hills wind away. I rolled down the window and rested my chin on the back of my hands on the car door, gasping and laughing as the wind snatched away my breath. My hair, so much shorter and lighter now, whipped around my head. I hadn't even bothered with make-up. Lately, I felt less like maintaining the pretense, more and more like coming out from under my wrappings. As if my tired old goth librarian identity had only ever been a mask hiding me from the sun and muffling my air. And although he hadn't said anything, I knew Edgar preferred me fresh-faced. He would frame my face in his hands and trace my cheekbones with his thumbs, looking into my eyes until I imagined we'd both vanished down some bottomless well.

I don't mean that metaphorically, not really. I was losing time more often now. It should have terrified me, but I couldn't seem to summon the energy for fear. I reassured myself that *losing time* was a rather hysterical description of what was only a general somnolence. Later I would describe it as the lovely drunkenness evoked by the bite of a vampire, a delicious heaviness seeping into the limbs and the mind and preventing the host from protesting the draining of their blood. I drifted through my hours in nearly perfect contentment, and every now and then, I woke up from a nap I hadn't meant to take.

Nearly perfect, because once in a while something would intrude and prick me into painful alertness. Evan would text me now and then with some random comment:

I've decided to start shelving Milk and Honey in the cookbook section. The food gods are less vindictive than the poetry gods.

Had a guy bring in a spiral-bound autobiography/marijuana growing guide he'd clearly printed off at home. Wanted it in the local authors section. I stuck it right on the shelf. How long do you think before Ned notices and loses his mind?

Ned was the head librarian now I was gone. His sense of humor—or lack thereof—was legendary.

The Daughters of the Confederacy are meeting in the conference room again. Remind me of the recipe for a Molotov cocktail?

You have to come back! Natasha keeps bringing her granddaughters in to meet me, and apparently there are roughly 72 of them.

Every time one of those messages buzzed in my pocket, it jolted me into an indefinable unease. Have you ever felt oddly uncomfortable all day and discovered too late it was because you'd buttoned your shirt wrong? It was like that. A niggling sense something didn't quite fit right. An irritant that gradually enflamed.

I'd try to text something back, something equally flippant and darkly silly, but I knew my words sounded stilted and cold. Evan's text messages came more infrequently as time ticked on. I pushed down the niggling inclination to simply block his number, put an end to this dissociative discomfort once and for all. I knew better than that, of course. It was always best to let these dangling relationships wither and die slowly rather than brutally uproot them.

Where did that come from? It wasn't as if I had a habit of ghosting friends. Right? Memories teased, drifting out of reach when I tried to grasp them. I shivered, even my skin suddenly unfamiliar and ill-fitting, rippling over my muscles and bones like rattling scales.

The uneasy feeling intensified when I looked in the mirror. I had stopped wearing makeup almost entirely. A bit of powder and lip gloss was all I bothered with if we were staying in. Going out was even easier, since wearing anything on my lips under a mask would have been ridiculous. Not to mention messy. I wondered how the lipstick manufacturers were doing these days.

I checked the case counts and death rates every day as the virus continued to spread its tentacles through the country and around the world. I felt like a spectator in the Colosseum, disinterestedly watching the pageantry of death as if it would never reach the seats. But in this circus, the dead were as likely to fall from a seat beside me as in the bloody sand below. Even as the crisis ballooned, as hospitals and makeshift field morgues overflowed, the days maintained their theater. My fascination with the numbers and the color-coded maps was the train wreck variety: I was happy to put my life on hold for a closer look at the wreckage and the gore, but I kept well off the tracks myself.

I hardly even worried about Edgar. Besides the reduced capacity, *La Table* had enhanced cleaning procedures in place and all the employees wore masks, all the time. There was no way to keep a six-foot distance in a working kitchen, after all. And everyone submitted to a temperature check at the beginning of their shift. It wasn't perfect, but it was as good as it could be. So far, no one from the restaurant had fallen ill.

Occasionally, I'd muse on how strange it was how this terrible virus that had so upended every facet of our lives was the one thing that had freed Edgar to be all mine and only mine, but most of the time Octavia felt like a long-ago ghost from a story I'd all but forgotten. Even wearing her nightgowns and sleeping in her bed and spinning her rings 'round on my finger couldn't make her more real. Edgar never said her name anymore. If it weren't for the photo album bearing her name, tucked safely away in that box, I might have wondered if she'd ever existed at all. If anyone really existed but Edgar and me.

You'd think I'd be bored, cooped up in the house most evenings by myself, but I wasn't. I'd put on a mask and walk up and down the streets in the chilly, fog-strewn nights. Sometimes I'd walk all the way to the restaurant and peer in the foggy plate-glass window like the Little Match Girl, but I never saw Edgar. He was back in the kitchen, of course. He'd often come home bearing tribute, some delicious confection, or a plate of appetizers, and we'd sit up together in bed, eating and drinking and laughing until we were too tired to stay awake any longer. I took to his schedule, sleeping in late and eating breakfast well past noon.

I found, much to my surprise, that I'd rather lost that path to peace through books. I'd always been an avid reader, but now my mind wandered, untethered by the words on the page. When I did force myself to pay attention, I'd wind up arguing with the writer instead of vanishing into the mind of the characters. All the stories felt artificial, and I staggered under the weight of every stone of plot laboriously laid on another.

I couldn't help wondering at all the time I'd wasted between pages. All the life I'd spent, ciphering out meaning from blotches of ink on dead trees, scribbled there by dead people with their dead ideas and dead quarrels and contentions and rivalries. How much spirit had I spent on make-believe, how many precious breaths squandered? Surely life was too short for such spendthrift.

My one indulgence remained with Devlin's letters. Even Octavia and Brigitte had lost their luster, their meager talismans easily brushed aside as I delved deeper into the psyche of Edgar's first love. They'd become nothing more to me than poor, faded copies, their outlines indistinct. I found myself reading Devlin's same letters repeatedly aloud, practicing what I imagined her inflection to be until I got it just right.

It seemed terribly unfair Devlin had died so young and so pointlessly. There was no poetry to her sort of death at all. I pictured how panic-stricken Edgar must have been when she collapsed on that high mountain trail. He'd told me how she'd gone from elated and determined to bag the peak when they'd started out in the chilly pre-dawn hours to irascible and argumentative. He'd tried to convince her to eat something, but she'd been irrationally furious at what she called his "mollycoddling," flinging the lunches they'd brought into the river. Less than an hour later, she'd gone down and hadn't opened her eyes again.

Edgar hadn't even been able to stay with her. They had no service there, so he'd dropped his pack and run up the trail as fast as he could until he wrangled a bar and called search-and-rescue. By the time he made it back, he had to start CPR on her. He hadn't been able to keep it up until the volunteers reached them two hours later, but I'm sure it wouldn't have mattered by then anyway.

She'd never been prone to talk much about the Type I diabetes she'd been diagnosed with only a year or so earlier. She resented the intrusion of the disease on her freedom and gave it as short shrift as possible. Edgar had seen her testing and poking herself, but he knew better than to ask too many questions.

Had she been deliberately pushing herself that day, determined to prove she was more than the disease, that she wasn't about to live her entire life at the whim of her pancreas? Or had she been a newly diagnosed young woman who lacked the experience with the disease to recognize the danger she was in? The truth might be simpler still: she was in denial of her own weakness and mortality.

I found myself suffering from the same denial. Devlin's writing was so immediate, so present, I could hardly believe myself she was dead. If anyone should have been able to fend off the Dread Specter by sheer willpower, it was her.

I wished I had Edgar's letters back to her. It was impossible to guess at his responses from reading hers. She was flighty, impassioned, and easily distracted, leaping from one idea to another, without regard to the reader. Emerging from her world, I felt giddy and exhausted at once, as if I'd been riding a carousel with a runaway engine.

As the stack of jasmine and vanilla-scented pages dwindled, though, she became obsessed with a single idea, and I realized—too late—she'd been anything but impervious to the reality of her own demise.

CHAPTER EIGHTEEN

Treasure,

You're right, of course. Not most of the time, but I'm gracious enough to grant you this once. I still refuse to be undone by something as mundane as cell decay.

What is the point of love if all it does is leave you vulnerable to the worst sort of misery in the end? People are so weak. So whiny! They live at the mercy of everything and take control of nothing and then cry foul when things don't go their way.

And things are NEVER going to go our way if we leave it up to Fate and the gods and chaos. They're shameless thieves, every one of them. They create nothing—they only manipulate and destroy what they can't understand. They're the worst sort of cowards. Incapable of love and feeding only on slavish adoration, they smash and smash and smash again.

Well, they're not going to smash us. We see them for what they are. And we know what we have for what it is—the one power that eludes them. They can't take it from us unless we surrender it. And I refuse to give an inch. I won't let you, either. You'll see.

Kitten

My heart thrilled as I read her words, and I found myself sitting on the edge of my chair, straining forward as if I could almost hear her voice, almost see the toss of her head, the glitter in her eyes. I couldn't decide if she was half-mad or entirely seductive. She wasn't a woman; she was a force.

I kept reading.

My treasure,

I think I'm figuring this out. I know, I know, you think I'm crazy. But I'm going to convince you.

Admit it, you want to be convinced.

I'm so tired of all these classes. I only spend about 10% of my time learning. The rest of the time I'm just taking up space, satisfying all their clichés and preconceptions about what a student should be. They like the idea of girls with long hair, carrying stacks of books under red-leafed trees, playing Greeks at stupid parties, and sharing deep thoughts with wise old professors.

I want to do. I want to make. I want to live and not plan to live.

Honestly, I wouldn't mind burning this whole campus to the ground if I thought society would burn along with it.

How do they all do it? Convince themselves they're happy? That they're successful. Satisfied. They're all blind slaves, merrily looping chain after chain around each other's necks, with their good credit scores and manicured lawns and shattered glass ceilings and PTA meetings. These are people who actually believe they're free because they're allowed to tick a box every four

*years. The whole system is cannibalistic, and they only
have children so they can begin feeding it.*

*I'm not going to play. They want us to believe it's
impossible to live, to really live. We have to get out of
here. Promise me you'll jump off this burning cliff when
I say jump.*

Your raging kitten

I burst out of my chair, veins roiling with energy that needed to go somewhere, anywhere. She was right. So much of what we thought were the necessities of happiness was only the trappings of servitude to a system that gobbled us all up.

Restlessness drove me outdoors, pulling a knit cap over my ears and tossing a scarf around my neck. The wind was drear and rain-driven, and I shoved my hands deep in my pockets as I walked, my head spinning with Devlin's words.

Everyone, I thought, felt that way deep down, knew in spite of themselves they lived in service to a lie. But it was so hard to fight against all the constructs. Most of us would rather quietly be devoured by our dog than risk being torn apart by wolves, even if it meant we lived our whole lives trapped in a kennel.

I wondered what Devlin would think of Edgar's life now. Would she approve? In some ways, Edgar certainly lived on his own terms. He never seemed to want for much in terms of money, though I wasn't clear on how that was possible. I didn't think he had family money, and surely chefs didn't make the sort of huge salaries that could easily weather terminal illnesses and restaurant closings. He'd sold his first restaurant after Brigitte's illness made running it impossible, so maybe that accounted for some of his wealth. Or maybe he just existed in a constant state of debt. It suddenly struck me as odd we'd never seriously discussed finances.

Edgar paid all our bills—I even handed over my phone bill

without a second thought every month. Money worries didn't seem to trouble him, so I'd all but forgotten to be troubled myself.

At any rate, Edgar was certainly well-stitched into the fabric of society. He owned a home, managed a successful restaurant, regularly gave interviews to local papers and magazines, and hosted all sorts of major events. Everyone in Forest Glen knew him, at least by reputation. He appeared equally happy strolling dark streets with me or watching TV or completing jigsaw puzzles. I was almost sure he was impervious to the painful discontent that had afflicted Devlin.

Of course, he wasn't just much older than he had been in those days—he'd suffered much more than the average adult had by the time they reached their thirties. Perhaps loss had softened him to quieter joys than Devlin would have permitted. She'd lived in a state of continual agitation, fighting invisible enemies who'd won in the end. Maybe Edgar chose a perpetual presence instead, eschewing both the agony of looking back and the terror of looking forward. That might be how he cheated Death: Edgar simply ignored it until the beast arrived, and then swept up and re-ordered his life after its departure.

An odd jealousy on Devlin's account took hold of me. How dare he seize the contentment that had so eluded her? How dare he build a life whose bricks were made of all the elements she most despised? She'd been so resolute their love would last forever. How dare he hold me and call me by the name that ought to have been only and always hers?

Always was a fiction, I told myself. Maybe the best testimony Edgar could give of the love they'd shared was to own it untouched and undiminished by however many lesser loves came later.

I'd so fallen half-in-love with Devlin myself by now, I wasn't even troubled to be one of those lesser loves. All I wanted was to get back to her letters, to lose myself in the incredible vivacity and vim of her words again.

But even this fancy couldn't quite drown out the question I'd finally gotten around to asking. When I returned to the house, I didn't go back to her letters. Instead, I went to Edgar's office, with its carved oak desk and two wooden filing cabinets stuffed with thousands of statements and menus and miscellaneous documents.

It took a few days to find what I was looking for. A strange terror had seized me, a terror shaped like curiosity. How had Edgar managed such an unworried existence? He was only thirty-two, the same as me. Multiple moves and not one but two sick wives, the loss of one business, and the unanticipated surge of a pandemic ought to have depleted just about anybody's reserves, if not driven them into outright bankruptcy. But Edgar was more than comfortable.

The answer, it turned out, was the obvious one. Substantial life insurance payouts from not just Brigitte and Octavia but even Devlin had made Edgar a very wealthy man. How strange, I thought, that the reckless and indomitable Devlin would do something as prosaic and practical as taking out a life insurance policy on herself at age twenty-one. And how much stranger that she'd named Edgar her beneficiary. They weren't even married.

They were engaged, though, I told myself. Surely a life insurance policy was just one of the many preparations one made for an upcoming wedding.

I then remembered something that should have been impossible to forget.

And even if it hadn't come to mind, I had the document in hand, with my name typed across the top line in thick black typeset.

I'd signed off on a life insurance policy of my own, naming Edgar the sole beneficiary. I hadn't thought anything of it at the time. He'd showed me the amendment he'd made to his policy, for an equally astoundingly high sum, naming me as his beneficiary. It had been one of many signatures I'd scrawled out, as he'd added me to his health insurance, to the deed on the house, to the title on his car.

I had so little to offer, from a financial viewpoint, I'd felt downright embarrassed by how easily and generously he made me his complete partner in life. I quite literally hadn't given the life insurance policy a second thought until just now.

I tittered uneasily, but the squeaky sound only intensified my anxiety instead of alleviating it.

What was wrong with me? Surely, I wasn't suspecting my own husband of plotting the murders of three women—*four*, my brain interrupted somberly, solely for financial gain. He did enjoy the finer things in life, I couldn't deny that. He had a great fondness for good food and wine, wore the most dapper of clothes, indulged in soft linens and intoxicating fragrances. But I'd never have described him as a greedy man, driven by the lust for money over all else. There was nothing wrong with indulging himself when he had the funds to do so.

But he'd gotten the funds from the bodies of his lovers, my brain piped up again.

Coincidence, I told myself firmly. The worst sort of luck. It wasn't as if he could fake breast cancer. And he hadn't even been in the room when Octavia died from the same virus that had taken tens of thousands of other lives.

Shame filled me. What sort of monster could even suspect him for an instant of such horrible deeds? I knew firsthand the grief he'd suffered when Octavia died. And he'd never shown me anything but the utmost kindness and devotion. He asked absolutely nothing of me in return but my love.

And that signature.

A hefty life insurance policy was only good sense, I argued, especially for someone who intimately knew all the ways death impoverished the bereaved. It wasn't just the cost of whatever illness had ravaged the dead or the exorbitant charges of funeral homes, with their boxes and urns and dirt and ash. It was all the lost days and weeks afterward when survivors were expected to pull themselves together and go to work and pay the bills as if they weren't fighting to breathe around a sucking chest wound.

No, I didn't begrudge Edgar a penny of the money he'd received for each of his losses. He'd used it, as money ought to be used, to make the unbearable survivable, to build a footpath out of the grave and back into the light. And if something ever happened to me, God forbid, I wanted to know Edgar could afford to simply walk away from the world we'd shared, that he could retreat to a safe place to mourn and remember how to live again.

How very adult of me, I thought drily, unsure if even I believed me.

I stuffed the papers back into their folder and closed the file drawer. I glanced around the room, trying to remember what I'd disturbed so I could hide any hint of my presence here. Edgar had never refused to answer any question I'd asked. I was sure he'd have told me about the life insurance policies on the other women if I'd thought to ask. And it wasn't as if he'd forged my signature on the life insurance policy he'd taken out on me or tried to hide what I was signing. I simply hadn't been interested at the time, hadn't assigned it the least importance.

I'd betrayed his trust by sneaking around behind his back, and I couldn't help compounding it by hiding the sneaking around itself. He deserved better from me, and I didn't want him to ever think for an instant I'd doubted him.

I'd feared him.

I shook my head. That was nonsense. It had been nothing more than a fleeting doubt, a silly suspicion fueled by too many murder podcasts and romantic suspense novels. Nothing could be more preposterous than me entertaining a moment's fear of the man who loved me more deeply than I ever could have imagined. The man I adored. Who even now, in all my shame and uneasiness and anxiety, I craved and hungered after.

And I was right. Edgar wasn't the one I ought to have feared at all.

CHAPTER NINETEEN

I didn't read letters in bed anymore. I reserved that indulgence for the hours Edgar was away. Our early morning hours were spent in slavish adoration of each other's bodies, murmuring secrets and making love and murmuring secrets again until sleep, at last, dragged us away. Even now, the sound of rain falling on a roof at night summons the taste of Edgar's skin under my tongue, the tensioned strength of muscles moving against my softness, the heated thrill of his breath whispering over my neck, my bare breasts, my open thighs. I have learned, to my sorrow, what it is to carry love into eternity.

I told myself I was playing dress-up, that these affectations of Devlin's I adopted more assiduously every day were nothing but a bit of theater. A means of reaching into Edgar's heart, of understanding all the secret canyons and arroyos of his soul. That somehow I might retrieve all the shredded parts he had lost when she died. If I wore her clothes long enough to learn her gait, he might no longer listen for her footsteps in the hall.

The truth was nothing so deliberate. Day by day, her words sunk further into my mind. I grew more impatient and irritable and impetuous and playful. I, who had never been inclined to walk much farther than to the bookstore or the bakery, began to spend my days on the winding, wooded paths whose trailheads began at the park on the edge of town. I strode along the damp earth with a make-shift walking stick, striking the wood on every stone in my way and singing out greetings to the chipmunks and jays I perturbed. I came home with twigs and leaves in my hair, fully frizzed out by the humid conditions, dirt on my cheeks, and little memory of where I'd been or how far I'd traveled.

The brain fog that had troubled me at its outset now scarcely registered. Plenty of people spent good money on weed and magic brownies to live in the same sort of happy haze. I felt stronger and healthier than I ever had. Alone, I was fearless and powerful; with Edgar, I lived in bliss and perfect security. As for the rest of the world—I hardly thought of it anymore. Even Evan had given up on disturbing me.

Devlin's letters, if you'd read them, might have seemed increasingly scattered and frenetic to you, but with the benefit of hindsight, her urgency was well-justified. Death stalked her, after all, whispering through her very veins, its bony fingers squeezing her organs tight, its breath mingling fermented-sweet with her own. Every day she warded it off with only a needle and a few precious drops of insulin. I couldn't blame her for obsessing over her most faithful companion, for panicking at the darkness staining the edges of every hour, for refusing to yield a single second.

She'd known what was coming. The late diagnosis of diabetes had rattled her. Unlike Type II diabetes, which could sometimes be managed with diet and exercise and occasionally a pill, Type I diabetes signaled a serious impact on her general health and her life expectancy. Even patients who followed every instruction lived significantly shorter lives than they otherwise might. Not to mention the constant poking and pricking and measuring and counting that must have weighed on a free spirit like Devlin's. Though she didn't mention her illness in her letters, I was sure she resented every restriction it created. And it was, after all, nothing more than a brief rebellion against those restrictions that had cost her life in the end. She'd been unwilling to acquiesce her own weakness, and the stubbornness that might have only resulted in fatigue and a headache for anyone else killed her.

Maybe stubbornness was the wrong word. Maybe it had been

an outright revolt. Maybe she'd seen the cliff looming ahead and rather than allow it to spell the end of her road, she'd taken that leap she spoke of.

So, when her letters spoke of what she termed *persistence*, it didn't strike me as odd. Someone so recklessly and fully alive would naturally have been unwilling to own the inevitability of death. Unwilling hardly described what had become an obsession to exceed the grave with the force of her will. She knew she couldn't carry her body with her—no scientist could deny the entropy of the flesh. But she was sure she could remain as conscious energy.

I'd long been a fan of the paranormal, both in my novel-reading and my pop culture indulgences. Nothing made me happier than a good ghost story. So I couldn't help rooting for her as I followed the trail of crumbs she'd left behind in her letters, hoping against hope she'd find a way to outwit the witch and return to the life she loved so well, stronger than ever. It wasn't until I got to the last letter that I belatedly realized just who would pay the cost of such a victory.

My dearest treasure,

You're not going to like this, but hear me out.

Without taking things into our own hands, we don't know when our bodies are going to give out on us. Some people blink out with just a little tap on the head, others linger for years with horrible diseases.

I've already told you I refuse to leave you behind just because a random electrical pulse fails somewhere. And it's so not my style to hang around like some sad ghost while the rest of the world keeps turning.

So I need you to choose a new host for me. Most people just drift through this life half-alive anyway. It's not as if we'll be stealing anything from them. If they're strong enough to resist us, then they deserve to keep their life as they choose. But you and I both know most people aren't so strong at all. They eat what they're told, drink what they're told, drive where they're told until they tumble into an open grave when they're told. If anything, we'll be doing them a favor. Granting them more life than they'd have ever experienced on their own.

It doesn't really matter what she looks like, as long as you find her attractive. It might even be fun to try out something completely different. I hope you'll be able to sense me nearby. I don't know. Despite all the stories people tell, there doesn't seem to be any hard data on spirits from the other side breaking through into this physical plane without some kind of catalyst.

The one thing you mustn't do is maintain some crazy celibacy on my part. You'll have to go through some sort of grieving period, just to maintain appearances, but don't waste any time. I think my ability to keep myself tethered here with you will weaken the longer I have to sustain myself without a body.

You pick her out, and I'll do the rest.

But this is a two-way street! You have to swear to do the same for me. If you tap out first, promise you won't go anywhere. I'll find you a body. I'll hold your place.

Let the sleeping stay asleep. You and me, we'll keep our eyes on each other.

You are my whole home, Treasure. Hold my place.

Kitten

The pages drifted to the floor beside the chair where I sat. Dazed, I stared at my limbs, my eyes following the black-and-red swirls and loops of ink as if I'd never seen my own tattoos before. Did Edgar believe this?

It was true he had a pattern of swiftly replacing his dead lovers. Did he truly imagine he was wooing a vessel for Devlin's ghost to possess? *Possess.* My brain tripped over the word, it was so preposterous, but what else could I call it? Was his devotion to me only vicarious?

Of course not, I tried to argue. Only a madman would believe such nonsense.

Obstinately, my brain dredged up uncomfortable details, like gin martinis and jasmine-scented lotions and a dead woman's satin-and-lace gown. If he'd been dressing me up like Devlin's voodoo doll, I'd certainly made it easy for him.

Why hadn't I protested? Was I truly as weak and vapid as Devlin thought everyone but herself, that I helped my husband indulge his pathetic delusion?

No more, I decided firmly. When Edgar came home tonight, I'd be waiting. And not with port wine and soft kisses.

CHAPTER TWENTY

Before Edgar got home, I made sure that when he came through the door, he'd see the woman with whom he'd first fallen in love, not some distorted reflection of a dead woman. I dug out one of my favorite outfits, a shameless cross between steampunk pirate and tavern wench. I couldn't do much about the lackluster color of my hair—I'd allowed it to mostly outgrow the black dye job—but I tied a couple of ragged pieces of black lace around two short ponytails on top of my head. I dug out my eyelash glue and carefully painted my lips a black-lined crimson.

I examined myself critically in the mirror. The woman staring back at me was no one's pale reflection. She was entirely, utterly herself.

She was also too damned hot for her own good. In spite of all my best intentions, when Edgar's eyes sparked and darkened as he took me in, I did not attempt to smother the answering flame in my belly. It wasn't until much later, when we both lay splayed and sated on our bed, that I forced myself to break our quiet euphoria.

I pushed myself up on one elbow so I could look into his face, telling myself I'd know if he lied to me. "Edgar, I have to ask you something."

He didn't open his eyes, but a little smile flickered untroubled on his lips. "Ask away, Kitten."

I winced but pushed on. "I finished reading Devlin's letters."

"Ah. She was something else, wasn't she?"

"She was that." I hardened my tone, determined not to lead up to my question, not to give him time to formulate what he thought I wanted to hear. "I need to know if you shared her delusion, if you chose me as some vessel for her to possess. If our whole marriage is just an extension of your obsession with a dead woman."

He raised his eyelids enough so his cool gaze could meet my eyes. "There is no *just*, Kitten. I chose you because I wanted you. And my Devlin couldn't be happier to breathe through your lips."

I couldn't move as he brushed his thumb over my mouth and palmed my bare breast. His words rasped over my flesh. "To feel my touch again, through your delightful skin."

Icy cold swept over me. His voice was so calm, so matter-of-fact. How could I not have known he was so hopelessly mad? Suddenly mobile again, I shoved myself back, my bare feet slapping on the hardwood floor as I instinctively grabbed the long, filmy silk robe to cover myself from his gaze. As I crushed the delicate fabric in my hand, I shuddered, remembering too late whose skin it had lately warmed. I dropped it on the floor, dug in the back of the closet for my ratty black fleece.

I'd thought I was prepared for this conversation. I thought I'd braced myself to hear the worst from his lips. But now he had blithely acknowledged what I most feared, my mind was spinning, scrambling to make sense of his words. And underneath it all, a terrible pain clutched at my veins, sent its agony rippling through my limbs.

He didn't love me. Couldn't love me. It had always only been Devlin for him.

I yanked the belt tightly around my waist and turned back to face him, though my knees trembled so badly I feared I might fall.

"You can't be serious," I protested, though I knew better.

Edgar sat up, unabashed by his own nakedness. My eyes couldn't help clinging to the ebony dusting on his swarthy chest, the wide swath of his muscular thighs. The beautiful body that had never been mine to claim, in the end.

For one crazy moment, my brain begged me to drop it. To

place my finger over his lips, to stop the words I'd never be able to forget. To go back to ignorance, to pretend for however long we had to live that the devotion with which he worshipped me was mine after all. What difference did it make what insanity his grieving heart believed if I could retreat into the safe haven of his arms and never leave?

All the difference in the world. Maybe I was as weak and pathetic as Devlin would have thought me, but I was still strong to demand I be loved for my own sake. To insist with all my weirdness and wildness and weakness, I deserved love undiluted by a longing after the dead.

"You know I'm serious," Edgar's voice rumbled gently over me as if every word wasn't a weapon. "You read her letters. You feel her, even now, moving with you. Moving in you. It's nothing to be afraid of. It's something beautiful. Something incredibly, impossibly rare."

Despair settled heavily with me. "I need a drink," I said abruptly, my voice cracking. "A damn *vodka* drink."

Edgar smiled as if he humored me. He followed me downstairs without bothering to dress. I poured icy vodka into a thimbleful of cranberry juice, drank it, and poured again. Even now, more than anything, I wanted to retreat into his embrace, tuck my head against his broad chest and listen to his heartbeat. I gritted my teeth.

"You've been gaslighting me," I said flatly. "It's not Devlin who's been haunting me, it's you. Fixing me her drinks, dressing me in her clothes, burning her damn flowery candles. Making me read her letters like it was some kind of gift when all you wanted to do was brainwash me into believing it could somehow be enough to be loved by a man who wants me to pretend to be a dead woman. What did Octavia think of that? Brigitte?"

Even as I said the words, I feared I already knew the answers. I remembered with sudden clarity the shifts in their personalities, the way they'd adopted Devlin's nickname as their own.

Edgar's eyes rested on me, full of pity. He reached for my hands, but I stepped back. "It's a lot to take in," he said. "That's okay.

It took Octavia and Brigitte a little while to understand, too. But they were much happier once they gave in. It's exhausting to fight against Devlin."

My heart cracked a little deeper to see his face light up as he spoke her name. "She's magic, Sigrun. She's so much more than any of us. Stronger. Braver. Let her take control. You'll be part of a love story any person would happily die to know. A love story that never ends."

The old suspicion crept back. "Did you kill them? Octavia and Brigitte? Is that what happened?"

Edgar sighed, shaking his head. "Of course not. I loved them. I loved Devlin *in* them. But her sort of resurrection comes at a cost. Two spirits in one body, even when one spirit sleeps, takes a toll. The body just can't last as long as it ought."

I jerkily opened the refrigerator and retrieved a lemon. I seized a santoku knife, sliced the lemon in half, and squeezed the juice into my third healthy glass of vodka. Fear and pain shifted inside me, making room for rage. "What the hell does that mean?" I demanded.

Edgar shrugged. "We're not entirely sure. The first time it took us by surprise. Devlin didn't know how to make sense of what she was feeling, and Brigitte went downhill much faster than anyone anticipated. I wasn't ready. Even though Devlin had succeeded once, I wasn't sure I believed she could pull it off a second time. I was hungry for every second I had with her, so instead of finding a new host, I spent every moment with Brigitte right until the end."

He spread his hands. My gaze narrowed, focusing on minutiae. The lifeline on his palm. The thatch of dark curls at the juncture of his thighs. A trickle of lemon juice on the marble counter. The delicate cobwebbing of the shattered ice in my glass.

"We did better with Octavia. This time she knew the warning signs. Her body was beginning to decay even before the pandemic hit. Neither of us was surprised when she fell victim to the virus. And this time, we were determined there be no delay. You remember the night she came to cooking class?"

"Valentine's Day," I answered dully, swishing the vodka in my glass and watching it leave little clear legs on the crystal.

"Yes. I wanted to get her blessing on my choice. You were quite a departure from her last vessel, but we both agreed it would be fun to try something a little out of the ordinary."

"And now what?" My gaze swung back up to meet his. Dear Lord, how could he look so rational?

"Now you let her all the way in. You've already done most of the work. Just surrender. It's painless, I promise. You'll sleep until it's time for your body to move on. Then you take over the last bit when she leaves. And just like with you, we'll have another vessel ready for her. Seamless."

I laughed—it was no more than a short, humorless bark. "You really think I'll help you pick another woman to betray me with?"

He had the temerity to look wounded. "Surely you remember we never slept together until after Octavia was gone? I've never been unfaithful to Devlin. Never once, since the day we met. And you—Sigrun—you'll be long asleep by then. Devlin will help me pick the next one."

Intoxication and grief swamped me all at once. I spared a moment's mourning for those other two women who had somehow lacked the will to resist this story of his, who'd given up their own identity and spent their lives pretending to be a ghost. Whose sense of self had been so deeply damaged, they truly believed it was better to be loved for how well they played another woman's part than to risk solitude as the women they were. How terribly sad it seemed. I thought my eyes might be wet.

This time, I allowed him to reach for me, his big hands wrapping around my wrists. My left hand held my empty glass. My right hand still clutched the santoku knife. In spite of everything, my eyes clung to his, searching desperately for my lover.

But he was gone. It was Devlin's lover who gazed so tenderly down at me, Devlin's lover who even now would sacrifice me without remorse to a specter he'd summoned out of nothing more than grief and madness.

Maybe I was as much like Devlin as he thought. I wasn't about to give death or despair a moment's quarter either.

"I love you so much, Edgar," I whispered. His eyes softened. His lips curved.

And now we're back to the moment when we first met, dear reader.

I plunged the knife into his belly. He didn't even have time to tighten his grip on my wrists. Glass shattered on the tile floor as I seized the slippery handle with my other hand and wrenched it across his stomach with all my strength, the blade dragging upward as he sagged, falling heavily against me.

We both fell to the floor, he on top of me. I scrambled to get out from under his weight, slipping and sliding in his blood, my bare foot catching in something I realized later was his spilling organs. I pulled the knife out with me, sent it spinning across the floor.

He didn't fight me. Maybe the damage and the blood loss was too catastrophic. Maybe he was simply in shock, too stunned to resist the death that galloped toward him. I was sobbing now, gasping, choking, my whole body shaking as if my bones would fall apart. I pulled his head into my lap, stroking his hair, his cheeks, with my bloody hands. His gaze burned into mine. No anger, no fear, no accusation.

Only a fierce, mad, endless love. "Hold my place," he gasped out hoarsely.

And his eyes closed.

CHAPTER TWENTY-ONE

Dealing with the aftermath was easier than you might think. Thanks to our vigorous lovemaking earlier in the evening, I had plenty of bruises and bite marks to offer the police as proof of being battered. Evan made a statement on my behalf attesting to how Edgar had isolated me, forcing me to give up my job and distancing me from my friends. I even told the truth about Edgar's "delusions," claiming he'd grown enraged when I refused to play the part of the departed Devlin, and I was forced to defend myself. And once all that settled, there was, of course, the half-million-dollar insurance policy Edgar had signed before we wed.

I cannot describe how strange, how surreal it feels to be on this side of death and its detritus after all this time. Sweet, silly Sigrun, with her leather-and-lace pretensions, her paltry darkness that never quite denounced the light, was at last driven utterly into a stupor by the horror and trauma of her own actions. I don't suppose I'll ever understand what drove her to such extremity. I didn't see it coming myself, and I was there.

It was a terrible shock, coming entirely into her body only to find myself watching my beloved Edgar fade out. I think I have had to focus so much on maintaining my own foothold here that I somehow forgot he, too, was susceptible to slipping away. I am almost ashamed to admit it, but for an instant there, as his lifeblood drenched my thighs, as his heart skipped and jerked and thudded, as darkness shuttered his beautiful eyes, I panicked. I howled like an injured animal, clutching his breathless head to my chest and begging, pleading with him to return.

But then I felt his hands, warm and strong, on my shoulders.

I couldn't see him, of course. Ghost stories are just that—stories for the stupid, the ignorant who know nothing of life and comprehend even less of death. I couldn't hear him. But I could feel him. And I remembered.

Hold my place.

Yes. Of course. My Edgar is not gone. My Edgar would never leave me.

I must allow some measure of time to pass. A token mourning period, at least. Enough to keep the jackals of this place at bay. I could move, of course, but I quite like this lovely haven Edgar has built for us here. Next time, then, we will try a new place. Costa Rica or South Carolina. Somewhere with warm beaches instead of cold rains and gloaming forests.

But for now, I am content in this dark and delightful corner of the country. So, I will begin my hunt here.

It's challenging, finding a new vessel in a pandemic, but I've always enjoyed a challenge. I dig through Sigrun's extensive cosmetics collection. She had a heavier hand than me, but no one could fault her colors for my purposes. I hollow my eyes, give my cheeks a wan complexion, carefully shadow my face with the faintest purple powders. A plain black cotton and lace mask covers the bottom half of my face. I brush my hair, newly dyed and lightened to a gleaming sunlit umber, and spray it into a cloud of waves drifting above my shoulders.

Perfect, I decide. Gorgeous and grieving, exactly the sort of bait to trap one of those savior-types.

I close my eyes and sigh, feeling Edgar's lips brush my forehead.

A new spate of virus cases has plunged the state back into harsher restrictions, but outdoor dining is still allowed. I tuck a book of Emily Dickinson into a pocket, grab my black umbrella, and head to the crepes-and-coffee shop two blocks away.

I spot him almost immediately. He strides up to the window, a sage green trench coat flapping around his long legs. Tanned skin tells me Oregon is not his native clime, and cropped, prematurely white hair makes his green eyes sparkle. He orders a large double cappuccino and sits a table away. He sits forward on the little metal chair that looks impossibly flimsy under his substantial frame, his eyes on the street. He is a study in leashed energy.

I like that. Quite possibly, like Sigrun, he will prove a little more difficult than the average person for my Edgar to subdue, but the win will be worth the battle.

He feels my gaze, turns his head to meet my eyes. I don't look away. I smile sadly and nod as if we are secret comrades. He smiles in return.

I will come back tomorrow, and so, I am sure, will he. It takes quite an effort to pick half-heartedly at the brie-and-mushroom crepes on my plate. I am suddenly starving. Suddenly happy. I want to run and laugh out loud at the sky.

Oh, Edgar.

We are almost there. I am holding your place.

THE END

ACKNOWLEDGMENTS

Many thanks to Lindy Ryan, who knows I can never resist a challenge and who delights in provoking me to the keyboard. This book also owes a huge debt to Toni Miller. She is a wicked chiropractor of the text and knows just which bones to twist and which ones to set in entirely different places. Monique Snyman kept my tendency to over-purple the prose firmly in check, and Najla Qamber's artist's eye brought the perfect cover to life, as always. Above all, I owe my gratitude to the readers and reviewers who spend their time and heart on my work.

And to the incomparable Daphne Du Maurier, whose ghost eyed me askance and whispered in my ear as I sat at my desk, I offer my eternal admiration

ABOUT THE AUTHOR

CASSONDRA WINDWALKER is the author of the novels *Idle Hands*, *Preacher Sam*, and *Bury the Lead*, in addition the full-length poetry collections *The Almost-Children* and *tide tables with god*. Her short-form work regularly appears in literary jouornals and wins the odd award, including the Helen Kay Chapbook Award for her poetry chapbook, *The Bench*. She has lived in the South, the Midwest, and the West, and presently writes full-time from the Frozen North. She keeps company mostly with ghosts, literary characters, unwary wild animals, and her tolerant husband. Twitter @windwalkerwrite